Contents

Killing Karma

By

Eldred Bird

Other books by Eldred Bird:

Catching Karma

Cold Karma

author@eldredbird.com

For Debi

Thank you for your patience and understanding.
Without it, this dream would never have been realized.

Chapter 1

Rose McCarthy, a simple straightforward woman in life, had no wish to be otherwise in death. The coffin she arranged to carry her earthly shell to its final rest appeared tasteful, but understated, the service short and to the point.

It was only 10:30 in the morning, but the late September sun had already taken its toll. The small group gathered at the cemetery on the western edge of the desert metropolis fidgeted, tugged at collars and ties, and fanned themselves with anything they could find. James stood in silence, his eyes fixed on his mother's casket, afraid to look away—like if he shifted his gaze for even one moment, it would become real. After what seemed an eternity, he straightened his back, swallowed the lump in his throat, and turned away.

The walk back to his car was only forty yards, but for James it might as well have been forty miles. His feet never broke contact with the ground as he trudged toward the parking lot, feeling as if his knees would give out at any time. A trembling hand produced the keys from his pocket and almost dropped them as he reached to open the door. He slid behind the wheel and stared at the passenger seat for a long moment.

The empty space grew as the memory of its former occupant echoed in his mind. Except for his mother, that space had never been filled by any other living being. No one filled it as he followed the ambulance carrying his mother to the hospital. No one filled it as he followed the hearse to the graveyard. Now it was filled only with memories. James found himself wishing there was someone else there, someone to fill the emptiness and break the silence on the long ride home. As he started the car and pulled out on to the street, he left her behind for the first time and, for the first time in his 31 years, James McCarthy was totally alone.

As he drove east toward downtown Phoenix, James found himself bypassing an onramp he would have taken on any other day. The I-10 freeway could have sped him home in a little over twenty minutes, but instead he opted to take the surface streets. He was in no hurry to get back to what he knew would be an empty house. His parents bought the house as newlyweds and his father renovated it with his own hands. Legally it belonged to James now, but in his heart it would always be theirs.

His entire life had been spent within the

walls of the little house located in the historic district west of Central Avenue. James recalled his earliest memory in the small, bright living room; it was a memory of his father. He could see a picture in his mind — just a snapshot frozen in time.

He recalled a large, dark haired man reaching down to pick him up. The man appeared so big and imposing, but his warm smile disarmed James and melted away any fears. He remembered the feeling clearer than the face . . . a feeling of warmth, and of love.

There were no other memories for him to draw on concerning his father. Everything else he knew about the man came from his mother, and she was reluctant to share. From what he could gather, John McCarthy died quietly in his sleep before James' second birthday. He always sensed his mother somehow felt abandoned by his father's passing, and she had never really forgiven him for leaving her alone.

It wasn't that she ever said anything negative about him, she just didn't say much at all. When James was old enough to start asking questions about the man, she gave only short, monotone answers — all facts and no feelings. He learned very young to stop asking.

James had been a late in life baby. His parents were married for some fifteen years before the arrival of their only child. His father worked in building maintenance at one of the larger hospitals in the area, and in his off time applied those same skills to the restoration of their home. His mother worked in the administration office of the same facility. When their eyes met for the first time, they both knew instantly what they had found. When his mother described the feeling as "soul mates" it was one of the few times James could remember hearing emotion in her voice.

After the passing of his father, Rose became very protective of James. Other than the days spent with an elderly neighbor while she worked, he couldn't remember more than a handful of times they had been separated.

The summer before James entered kindergarten his mother left her job at the hospital and went to work in the front office of the elementary school he would be attending in the fall. At the time he thought she did it to help him with the transition to this next stage of his life, but later came to understand it was for her peace of mind, not his.

Every morning they arrived at the school together and on most days, shared lunch in the office. After classes were over and the other children left the grounds by bus, car, bicycle, and their own feet, James would make his way to the office where he sat quietly and worked on whatever project had been assigned to him. If he had no homework, he wrote stories, drew pictures, or just got lost in his own thoughts. When Rose finished her duties, they left together, made the short drive back to the little house, stepped inside, and shut the door on the outside world for the night.

James continued driving along the busy streets watching people go about their business. Passing a school, he saw several groups of students talking and poking at each other as they walked between classes. The scene made him think about how he continued to shut that door on the world.

James carried the isolation of his early childhood into his high school years. He chose to eat his lunch alone, spending his free hours in the library. As he had done in the past, he spent most of that time writing. If something sparked his interest, he did hours of research, compiled his findings, wrote about how he would approach the experience and then . . . nothing. He would tuck the document into his ever-growing notebook, walked home, and shut that door. At the time, this writing exercise seemed pointless. Little did he know it would set him directly on the path to his current career.

In his senior year James took a journalism

class. As the class ended one day, the teacher noticed James' now bulging notebook. Mr. Jessup called for him to stay behind as the other students filed out of the room.

"Have a seat, Mister McCarthy." He pointed at the binder. "Do you mind if I have a look at your work?"

Without a word, James handed over his private collection. He sat, head hung low, while the man thumbed through the hundreds of pages.

After some time had passed the teacher closed the cover, removed his glasses, cleared his throat, and spoke very deliberately to the shrinking figure before him.

"Do you have any idea what you have here, son?" he asked.

James had a sinking feeling in his stomach. With his head still hung low he replied in almost a whisper. "It's just some stuff I wrote. I did it on my own time, Mr. Jessup. Really . . . I haven't been doing it in class, I swear."

"Mr. McCarthy," he said, leaning forward and placing a hand gently on James' shoulder. "What you have here is a future."

James raised his head, and for the first time made contact with the smiling eyes looking back at him. The sinking feeling faded, replaced by a warmth he had felt only once before. It was the same feeling he had when his father reached down to pick him up.

Mr. Jessup continued. "You have a gift, James. Your research is thorough, your conclusions are solid, and your style is clean. I think people would enjoy reading some of these articles."

The next thing out of the man's mouth caught James by surprise.

"With your permission, I'd like to show a couple of these to a friend of mine. He owns an agency that supplies filler articles to magazines and newspapers."

James replied with a little excitement in his voice this time. "Really? I . . . I mean, yes. Yes, please."

"Now I can't promise anything, but I'll talk to him." His teacher removed a few pages and handed the notebook back. "He might want to see more, or maybe have you write something from scratch. Can you do that?"

"Yes sir." James spoke a little quieter this time. "Will I be graded on it?"

Mr. Jessup let out a little laugh. "No son, you will be *paid* for it if he uses it. That's what I meant about a future. You might be able to make a living doing this, or at the very least, help your mom with the bills."

James caught himself smiling as he thought about that day. The introduction had indeed led to a career. Mr. Simon J. Walker, owner and sole proprietor of Walker and Associates, was impressed enough to buy several articles from him that school year. To this day, Mr. Walker was still providing James with a steady flow of work.

Several times a day, he received emails from Simon with topics requested by his regular clients. Sometimes he also included suggestions for subjects currently considered hot. These were articles that might be easy to sell and could be written on speculation. James responded to the messages, usually with articles attached, and the next week a deposit showed up in his bank account.

The subjects ranged from a compilation of the latest cell phone reviews to a detailed tutorial on how to survive a polar bear attack in the Yukon. James wrote them all, but his favorites were the travel guides. He researched every detail, imagined himself in the most exotic of places, and then wrote as if he had been there.

These tended to be his best-selling articles. His colorful language and poetic descriptions had a way of transporting the readers. As they read, they could feel the wind in their faces and the sand between their toes. When James McCarthy traveled, he took you along for the ride. Well, *Josh McDaniel* did.

Josh McDaniel was the pen name James used when he wrote. In the beginning, he feared seeing his own name in print. He felt if the people who knew him saw the stories, he would be ridiculed. After all, what could he possibly know of the world? James had never been anywhere or experienced anything outside of a forty-mile radius centered on that house in downtown Phoenix. Josh was free to travel and live a life of adventure, while James stayed home, tethered to his computer. Josh was worldly, wise and experienced — James was not.

Wearing the virtual mask of Josh, James could live out his dreams, if only in his writings. His avatar trotted the globe seeking adventure and reported back to the waiting readers of various travel magazines and websites. The stock photos inserted by Simon added flair and another level of credibility to the tales.

Josh's travel escapades received more positive reviews than anything else James wrote. Their popularity compelled Simon to compile the lot of them into several books. The travel anthologies sold fairly well in the electronic format, with a good number of printed copies being ordered as well.

James wasn't getting rich off his writing, but he made a decent living from it. It provided enough to pay the bills and take care of his mother when she was forced to stop working due to her health, and he managed to build a decent savings account as well. James saw to it they had a comfortable existence, but again, an isolated one.

This virtual job allowed him to work completely from home. He left the house for very little beyond taking Rose to appointments or doing the food shopping. As for most of their other needs, he became very proficient at sourcing things online and having them dropped directly on the doorstep—the same doorstep he now approached as he turned the car into the narrow driveway.

James put the vehicle in park and set the brake, as he always did. The lump returned to his throat as he surveyed the neatly trimmed greenery surrounding the pale, yellow structure. Everything looked the same as he had left it, and yet different. The plants were the same, the color the same, even the dark wooden front door remained the same . . . but different. He questioned whether he had the courage to go through that door alone.

What would Josh do? He thought to himself.

Swallowing the lump in his throat, James

walked slowly toward the house. He unlocked the door and turned the handle. He knew as he opened the door, he was opening a new chapter in his life.

Chapter 2

The morning sun streamed through the kitchen window as James finished drying and putting away the last of the breakfast dishes. There were no more than you could count on one hand, but he still felt compelled to stick to Rose's rules when it came to keeping things clean. Neither of them left the room as long as there was a dirty dish in the sink, or the counters were not cleared and properly wiped down. In her mind a dirty kitchen would lead to mice and bugs, and that was not going to happen in her house and in James' mind, it was still her house.

In the months since her passing, he hadn't changed a single thing or even moved it from its appointed position except to vacuum and dust. After cleaning an area, he took great pains to make sure everything was put back in exactly the same divots in the carpet or worn spots on the tables and shelves. These cleaning sessions always happened on the same schedule. James and his mother developed a routine and he was afraid to break it. He even felt compelled to maintain Rose's bedroom to the same standard since her passing.

After putting away the last dish and neatly hanging the towel on its rack to dry, James made his way to the small, dark den, sat down in front of his computer, and hit the power button. The screen came to life and his window on the world opened once again. He relaxed and settled in, ready to leave himself behind for the day. This was where James McCarthy ended, and Josh McDaniel began.

James clicked on the email icon and watched as the pile of spam filled his inbox. Scattered in between were several emails from Simon Walker. He changed the sort option so they would group together, then blocked the lot and pulled them into his 'Work' folder. He scanned for any other important messages, sorting them into the proper folders as well, and flushed everything else. This routine happened no less than three times a day. Like the counters in the kitchen, James kept his mailbox spotless.

After the passing of his mother, James continued to pursue his career without a break. Simon offered to take him off the assignment list for a while, but James wouldn't hear of it. Instead, He stepped up the pace of his writing.

Not having to take care of his mother meant he had more time on his hands. More time on his hands meant he had more time to think. The one thing James did *not* want was time to think. He thought about his life, a life that as far as he could see, added up to nothing. He escaped the nothing in his life by writing, and when he put on the persona of Josh, James felt he was something.

James clicked on the 'Work' folder and opened each message one by one, responding to Simon with blurbs that were short and to the point: Yes, I'll write this one. No, please give this to someone else. Please see the attachment and let me know if this meets your needs. The process continued, as it normally did, until James hit a bump in the road.

"This can't be happening!" He said out loud as he read the body of the letter again.

Dear Mr. McCarthy,

I am writing to make a special request of you. The editors of several travel publication and websites will be attending a local conference in March and are requesting an audience with Josh McDaniel. They would also like to discuss the possibility of speaking engagements and public appearances.

Per our agreement, I have not disclosed the author's true identity; however, these are very important people in our industry and are regular purchasers of your work. I fear if you refuse to meet with them, it may impact any future sales of materials under the Josh McDaniel name.

I realize this may put you in a difficult position, but your true identity can only be protected for so long, as the popularity of Mr. McDaniel is on the rise. I would suggest that we take this opportunity to release the information while we still have control of the

James was already spending more time in 'Josh mode,' but this letter changed everything. Lately, in addition to researching and writing more articles than normal, James was also spending a considerable amount of time going back through old files and rereading them. He found himself looking at Josh less as a mask to hide behind and more as another person, a person he could look up to.

Josh had so much knowledge and experience. He had been to countless places and done so many things. From zip-lining through the rainforest canopy in Costa Rica to starting a life saving fire with nothing but sticks and a pocketknife, Josh had done it all.

Josh became so real to James he even started building a picture of him in his mind as he wrote. He imagined a tall dark-haired man, muscular but not over built, with a few tattoos accenting his well defined arms. His tanned skin also bore some faded scars, chronicling the many adventures he had come through victorious, but not completely unscathed. James saw Josh as a man's man and every woman's dream.

In contrast, James was of average height and a proper healthy weight, with neatly trimmed mousy brown hair. He spent so much time inside that his skin was pale and un-weathered. He bore no scars and had never even peeked through the window of a tattoo parlor, let alone ventured in. His clothes were clean, pressed and showed no signs of wear. James always looked like he was just getting ready to go out, but he rarely did. When he looked in the mirror, he had to admit he was a little jealous of his own creation. But now he needed to *become* Josh, and that was a tall order.

James read through some of the articles and tried to use his imagination to put himself in the stories. Every time he painted a picture in his mind it was not his own clean-cut figure he saw, but the rugged unshaven form of Josh McDaniel that materialized. He closed his eyes tight and tried to force the image into submission, but the dark-haired specter would not go away. James came to the conclusion that for better or worse, Josh was here to stay. The two of them needed to find a way to coexist, and possibly become one.

James began trying to think of ways to make the merger happen. As inspiration took hold, he sat up straight at his computer, opened a new document, and started typing. He titled this new work "The Differences Between Josh and James."

He lost track of the time as his hands flew over the keyboard. Words seemed to be falling out of his brain while his fingers did their best to funnel them onto the screen. When the flurry of activity subsided, he was left with two columns stretching over the length of a half dozen pages.

As he ate lunch, he began to process the fruits of his labor. The first thing to become clear was that James never colored outside the lines. Things were very black and white in his world and he always seemed to "do the right thing." His mother had insisted on it.

Rose taught him he should always do the right thing for the right reasons, even when no one is watching. She called it her golden rule. While not religious, she believed the universe always had an eye on you. If you did bad things, bad karma would circle back and find a way to make you pay in the end. James concluded that if good karma worked the same way, he must have a lifetime of it banked already.

Looking over the other side of the balance sheet, he noted Josh spent more of his time in the gray areas. While he never really did anything blatantly wrong, he was always pushing the boundaries of societal norms, never considering the consequences of his actions. James figured the only reason nothing ever came back to haunt Josh was because he didn't really exist. The only way karma was going to get its teeth into Josh's behind was if *James* wrote it that way.

In a way, he felt a little empowered by the thought. Maybe the key to living with Josh was to recognize he was in control of him. Josh owed his very existence to the man sitting in front of the keyboard . . . or was it the other way around?

The character of Josh allowed James to make a good living. James figured their relationship was a little like the relationship between a ventriloquist and his dummy. Each owed their success to the other, but in the final analysis they were a team and needed to work together as one. The thought of Josh as the dummy brought a smile to James' face.

James felt he now had a better grip on their alliance. The next question was what to do with the knowledge. James came to the conclusion he couldn't go on existing the way things were. As much as he found comfort in sticking to the routines he and his mother developed over the years, he wanted more. Josh seemed to be the key.

Maybe, he thought, *it's time to forget some of 'Rose's Rules' and start taking a few lessons from Josh.*

James immediately felt guilty for letting the thought enter his head. What would his mother say? He knew exactly what she would say. Her statement would no doubt be delivered in a clear stern voice, but the thought of his mother's disapproval wasn't enough to drive the idea from his mind. This was his life now. He needed to take control and make some changes, and he only had a couple of months to do it. If straying from the narrow path he currently walked was the answer, then so be it.

The next logical question was how? How do you change a lifetime of proper behavior and putting others first? James couldn't see himself making a hard, left turn and setting off in a new direction. He turned to Josh, looking for an answer. What would Josh do?

Just like the ventriloquist's dummy, Josh had the power to do and say things James couldn't get away with. He had to find a way to become more like Josh.

James pondered the question the rest of the day, finding it difficult to concentrate on his work. Everywhere he looked he saw the figure of the rugged adventurer. Josh stood by and watched when he took out the trash or changed a load of laundry. When he typed on his computer, Josh spoke the words on the screen. At one point, James swore he saw the man napping on the couch.

How do I become Josh? He thought.

That was the million-dollar question.

After watching the evening news, James decided the best thing to do was sleep on it. He put the last of the dinner dishes in the cupboard, turned off the lights, and retreated to his bedroom. He completed his usual nightly routine, slipped under the covers of the neatly made bed, and closed his eyes. James was determined to make some significant changes to his life . . . tomorrow.

***

"Editing!" James blasted out of a dream and sat straight up in bed. *"That's the answer I'm looking for!"*

Editing was something he was very good at. The secret to good editing wasn't to throw out the whole piece if he didn't like it. The process was to make a small change and reread the text, repeating the action until he achieved the desired result. He needed to edit *himself* with an eye toward Josh. He could make small changes, one at a time, see where it took him and then build on it.

Having a plan gave James the relief his troubled mind needed. He closed his eyes once again, waiting for sleep to come.

Tomorrow, he thought, *I'm going to that 'Bank of Good Karma' and make my first withdrawal.*

Chapter 3

The next few nights James slept a little better. Though he still had not responded to Simon's request, he was becoming more comfortable with the idea of change. He even left the previous day's breakfast dishes in the sink until lunchtime. While not an earth-shattering moment, it was a step in the right direction. In truth it bothered him all morning, even to the point of disrupting his ability to concentrate on work, but he did it anyway.

Baby steps, he kept telling himself. *Just keep taking those baby steps.*

James settled in at his desk and pulled out his "Differences" list. The document had been stapled neatly in one corner and given it its own file folder in the drawer. Looking at the list was already becoming a morning ritual. He underlined things that stood out and made notes. Painfully aware of the major differences between himself and Josh, he decided to focus on the small differences first—the things he might more easily integrate into his own life and personality.

Once again referring to his editing analogy, James reasoned a small change in punctuation could sometimes make the biggest difference. Without changing any words, punctuation could change the entire meaning of a sentence or paragraph. What differences between him and

Josh would meet that qualification? Punctuation could be used to emphasize something or make it stand apart from its surroundings. He felt he could definitely use some emphasis.

The first thing that made Josh standout in his mind was the way he imagined the man looked. He figured if they entered a bar together all eyes would be on Josh, while he just faded into the wallpaper. James had never been in a bar.

Do bars even have wallpaper? He thought.

Then again, maybe he would be the one sticking out like a sore thumb while Josh fit right into the scene. Either way, his look seemed like a logical place to start.

James leaned forward, fingers on the keyboard, and readied himself to type. He felt compelled to do more analysis and come up with changes he could easily make to his outward appearance. Maybe he could change his clothing or get a new hairstyle. He stopped without typing a word.

Josh wouldn't make a list, he thought. *He would go with his gut and throw on something like his favorite jeans and a comfortable, worn t-shirt.*

James sighed. He owned neither. His casual wardrobe consisted mostly of sharply creased Dockers and meticulously ironed, button-down shirts. His only t-shirts were the crisp, white ones he wore underneath his other clothes. James knew it was time to go shopping.

So, where does one go for comfortable, broken-in clothes? James started the shopping trip in his usual way—on the internet. It didn't take him long to figure out this job was going to require a different approach. He needed to venture out into the *real* world. The job also required another step he wasn't sure he was ready for—shopping in secondhand stores. A picture of his mother sitting straight up in her coffin popped into his mind.

Rose McCarthy, though frugal, never condoned shopping in thrift stores. The whole idea of wearing another person's clothes sent shivers up her spine. It didn't matter how many times you washed something or how much soap you used, the thought of someone else's filth could never be scrubbed away.

And the shoes . . . don't even get started on the shoes. You'd have thought by her reaction even trying them on would cause your feet to rot off, leaving only stumps behind. James figured he could handle the clothes. As for the shoes, well, he could just scuff up a pair of his own for now.

Considering the possible shopping venues in his own neighborhood, James concluded it wasn't the best place to wade into the used clothing pool. While his street appeared clean and relatively well kept, the same could not be said for some of the surrounding areas. To the east and the south of him, things got downright scary. These areas were known more for gangs, drugs and a large homeless population. He did not expect to find anything Josh, or he for that matter, would wear in that part of town.

He thought the more affluent areas like Scottsdale and Paradise Valley would be a better place to start. Maybe the clothing, while previously worn, would be of a little better quality, as he assumed the people donating it were.

His mother still never would have approved, but she wasn't here anymore. He kept telling himself Rose's rules don't apply. Josh was his shopping companion today. When he looked in the mirror at the end of the day, he wanted to see Josh standing over his shoulder giving him the thumbs up, not his mother.

Putting the list back in its folder, James prepared himself mentally for what lay ahead. Like it or not, he was about to be thrust out of his comfort zone and into new territory. The thought of mixing with the unwashed masses made his skin crawl, but he didn't let that stop him. James picked up his keys, put on his best "Josh" face, and walked out the door.

A quick twenty-minute drive brought him to his first thrift shop experience. Walking through the door, the realization hit him; this was *not* going to be his typical shopping trip.

The first thing to jump out was the smell. It wasn't the crisp linen and perfume smell he encountered in the department stores he occasionally shopped in with his mother; it reeked of something a little more . . . well . . . old. The smell reminded him of the house where the aging neighbor lady used to care for him while his mother worked. It made the hair on the back of his neck stand up.

The next assault to his senses came in the form of several children, screaming as they ran up and down the aisles chasing each other, touching everything in sight. James froze in place when one of their pink, sticky hands came within an inch of his clean, pressed trousers as the child ripped past. The look of horror on his face must have been something. His reaction prompted the mother to deliver a sharp verbal response followed by a head slap to the offending minor.

James caught himself whispering under his breath as he pulled a shopping cart out of the rack. "Toto, we're not in Kansas anymore."

He felt like he already had a close encounter with the flying monkeys, and the woman behind the register? Well, she bore a striking resemblance to the Wicked Witch of the West. Parts of the store looked like they had been hit by a tornado and a skinny, tattered figure stood hunched over a bin, digging through odd socks—Scarecrow maybe? James found himself looking for the Cowardly Lion and the Tin Woodsman as he made his way through the racks to the men's pants.

The section of jeans was large, but he quickly found the size selection to be very hit or miss. The condition also varied from almost new to what he considered quite disgusting. One pair of pants contained more voids than fabric. A few strategically placed stains led him to question the personal hygiene of the previous owner. James pulled out a small bottle of hand sanitizer and used it before continuing on to the next rack.

He did manage to find two pairs of slightly faded, but generally acceptable jeans in what appeared to be his size. He decided to try them on. Looking toward the back of the store, he spied the fitting rooms. James' stomach twisted.

Three plywood stalls with a thin coat of dirty white paint stood in one corner. Each was adorned with what looked like saloon doors covering only the area from just below the knee to about chin height. Two of the three sets of doors hung crooked and gapped slightly. James recoiled in fear. He already had several firsts under his belt today. He didn't want to add exposing himself in public to the list.

New plan, he thought to himself. *I don't need to try anything on. I'll just buy the stuff and if it doesn't fit, I'll donate it right back and try again.*

He knew his mother would have lectured him about wasting money, but then she never would have been here in the first place, so the point was moot. The new plan also gave him a chance to wash the clothes one more time before they touched his skin. That comforted him and gave him the courage he needed to allow his shopping to continue.

Courage, he thought. *Maybe I'm the Cowardly Lion.*

James headed for the shirt racks, dodging the flying monkeys one more time.

There were several rows of shirts numbering in the hundreds, no two alike as far as he could tell. Seeing as how most of his current wardrobe consisted of solid color button-down shirts, he chose to avoid that section. The move eliminated about twenty percent of the garments, helping to narrow his search.

Next were the T-shirts. He just couldn't see himself wearing something advertising beer, proudly espousing the virtues of being a redneck, or bearing a slogan like "Give Peas a Chance." Avoiding T-shirts with writing on them cut the selection by another thirty percent.

Next in line were the polo shirts. They had collars and still sported a few buttons. He reasoned it was acceptable to wear them with jeans, either tucked in with a pair of loafers, or un-tucked with sneakers. James caught himself talking out loud. "Now we're getting somewhere, Josh."

He quickly snapped his head around to see if anyone heard him address his imaginary friend. It seemed his slip had been covered by the loud, dry coughing of Scarecrow, who now fumbled with the shoes lining one wall.

James found several unstained polo shirts in various colors and states of wear. He also picked out a light gray, long sleeved Henley, deciding with some trepidation that not everything had to have a collar. He felt a little braver as he shopped, even picking out a red and gray flannel shirt. The soft fabric reminded him of a warm hug, something he didn't have too much experience with, but the thought made him smile.

As James wheeled his bounty toward the front of the store, something on the end cap of an aisle caught his eye. It was a jacket. This wasn't just any jacket, but a faded brown bomber style jacket. He touched the sleeve, pulling back quickly as if he had just been shocked.

Real leather! He thought. *Not vinyl or fabric, but real, butter soft, worn-in leather!*

He reached out again and ran his hand over it. He could feel its history in the scuffs and stitches. James swore the jacket was speaking to him. He couldn't help himself. He freed the garment from its hanger and slipped it on right there in the middle of the store. It fit like it had been custom tailored to fit his frame.

Now that's what I'm talkin' about!

He could hear Josh's voice like the man was standing right next to him.

Don't look at the price tag. Hell, don't even take the damn thing off.

James turned and looked in the mirror and that's when he saw it for the first time. There, behind the dirty handprints and scratched glass he saw a new man—and Josh McDaniel stood right behind him with a huge grin and both thumbs extended skyward.

Chapter 4

James felt energized by his recent shopping trip. He even stopped at a mall on his way home to get a few accessories to complement his "new" outfits. After his otherworldly adventure in the thrift store, the mall pretty much lost its intimidation factor. He surprised himself when he entered through the main doors instead of slinking in the side entrance.

The leather jacket inspired him to go a little further with his makeover than he'd originally intended. He picked up a comfortable pair of hiking boots and a rugged, oversized watch with a studded leather band. He figured the thin, sleek dress belts he normally wore wouldn't fit too well with the boots and jeans, so he picked out a wide, black leather one with a large, but not too over the top bronze buckle.

When he tried on a pair of aviator style sunglasses, he could hear Josh's voice in the back of his head.

Pull back on the reins, Buddy. You're pushin' this horse a little too hard.

"Josh . . . the voice of reason?" He muttered to himself. "What's the world coming to?"

James was on an adrenalin high. His boundaries were being seriously pushed, but for some reason he found himself enjoying it. He couldn't help but smile as he stood in his bedroom, surveying the fruits of the day's labors. Everything was freshly washed, dried and laid out neatly across the bed in preparation for his fitting session. He managed to resist the temptation to break out the iron even though he found it physically painful.

He also took another big step. James moved the antique, full length mirror from its assigned corner in his mother's room. It now stood next to his closet, ready to give him a head-to-toe look at the final product of his editing. It wasn't exactly redecorating, but he took it as a sign he might be moving closer to a time when he would be able to make the house his own.

He stripped down to nothing but his underwear and socks and stood in front of the mirror. He paused for a moment, taking in the pale figure looking back at him.

I can't believe I'm doing this, he thought to himself.

"Believe it!" The answer came back from the man in the mirror. It took a second for the startled James to realize the voice he heard was his own.

He opened his mouth again. "Great. Now

I'm talking to myself . . . and answering."

James looked around the room, like he expected to see someone else waiting to comment on the state of his sanity, but he was alone. The man in the mirror had been the only witness to his transgression. With no one to question his mental state, it was time to start the transformation.

The first thing to touch his body was a pair of jeans. They were the foundation of his new look. Like the foundation of a house, he would build on them to create a solid image.

As he pulled on his first pair of blue jeans ever, a look of surprise came over his face. He expected them to feel rough and scratchy, but instead they felt soft and strong at the same time. It was a strange feeling and completely unexpected, like putting on a comfortable suit of armor. As he looked at himself in the mirror, shirtless and half clad in denim, he experienced what could only be described as physical reaction. Without thinking, James raised his arms and flexed his muscles.

He turned beet red with embarrassment as the realization of what he had just done settled in. *That was a total Josh move,* he thought to himself. He grabbed a faded royal blue polo and pulled it over his head. Brushing his hair back into place as best he could with spread fingers, he checked his reflection once more. *Better.*

James tucked his shirt in and threaded the wide belt through the loops as the crimson continued to fade from his face. Buckling the new watch around his wrist, he sat on the edge of the bed, pulled on his boots, and laced them up.

As he stood up, he placed a hand on the leather jacket, gripped it by the collar, and donned it with a flourish like a superhero putting on his cape. He felt the power flow through him again, the same power he felt when he first touched the jacket in the thrift shop. James straightened his back and stood a little taller.

Stepping in front of the mirror once again, he inspected the man standing before him. He started at floor level and slowly moved his eyes upward, taking in each detail along the way. As his gaze reached shoulder level he hesitated. Everything he saw so far matched the picture he painted in his mind, but what about the final piece?

When he continued upward, James fully expected to see Josh's face sitting on top of the shoulders, but the eyes he met as he raised his head were his own.

James stood motionless for a moment but couldn't contain himself any longer. A huge smile broke out across his face. The quiet, conservative well pressed young man that started this journey was gone. The figure before him now appeared quite different. This man stood a little taller, a little straighter and had an air of confidence about him. His hair was tousled and the eyes that used to look back at him with an empty stare seemed to sparkle a little. And the smile . . . the smile was something he had *never* seen before.

James spoke out loud once more. "Whoever said the clothes make the man knew what he was talking about." He looked himself up and down one more time. "Ok, Josh. We did a good a job on this edit. What's next?"

Well, kid, James could hear Josh's voice in the back of his head. *You've got the look now, but those clothes have a lot more experience than you do.*

The smile faded from James' face as he stroked a worn spot on the sleeve of the jacket. Josh was right; James had no experience to speak of. Everything he knew came through the monitor on his computer or the screen of his TV. Even this jacket had seen more life than he had. He imagined every sign of wear told a story — a story he was not a part of.

Josh spoke once again.

You need to get out and make some of your own stories, kid. Get some sun on your face, meet some new people and collect a few scars. Don't just edit your look, edit your life. Hell, get a life to edit!

James deflated as he sat back down on the bed, his shoulders returning to their usual slumped position.

Get a life.

The words echoed in his head and punched deep into his gut. For the first time, those words really sunk in.

Get a life.

He spent his entire youth either alone or with his mother simply existing, but not living.

Get a life.

James felt sick.

"How," he wondered. "How do I even start?"

Josh didn't speak. No sage advice or words of wisdom came pouring out as they usually did. With his internal mentor at a loss for words, he felt even more alone. Not only had he learned to live with Josh, but he also relied on him now. He considered Josh his compass on this journey, and the one with the map.

How would Josh approach this? James tried with everything he had to listen for his inner voice. No answer. He felt confident after his thrift shop experience, but where was that feeling now? The clothes transformed him physically and he had hoped, mentally as well. He placed his hand on the jacket again and closed his eyes for a moment, reliving the day's events and trying to recapture that feeling.

After a few minutes of contemplation, James took a deep breath and pulled his shoulders back as he stood up. He spoke out a little louder this time.

"I don't need Josh! Josh only knows what *I* wrote for him, so I know what *he* knows!"

That's the spirit, Jimmy boy!

Josh was back.

The clothes don't make the man, the man makes the man. You are what you do, so get out there and do something!

That seemed to be the answer James sought. Just get out there and do something . . . anything. It didn't have to be some grand adventure right out of the gate, and he didn't need to have a plan, he just needed to go out that door and start walking. Experience was not going to come to him, he had to go to it. His new life waited for him on the other side of that door.

James picked his wallet up off the dresser and slipped it in his pocket as he stepped out of the bedroom and walked down the narrow hall. When he reached the living room he paused and faced the big wooden door. A lump formed in his throat. Why did going through it feel so much harder than when he left for the thrift store? It was just a door.

That door had always kept the world out

and made James feel safe, but now it kept him in. Once his bodyguard, it now felt more like his jailor. The time had come to break out of his self-imposed prison and see what the world had to offer. James took a step forward, pulled his keys from their hook, and released himself.

As the door closed behind him, he swore he heard Josh again.

Look out world. Ready or not, here comes James McCarthy!

Chapter 5

The streetlights buzzed to life over James' head as the sun set behind him. Nerves got the best of James as he walked east toward Central Avenue. His eyes darted back and forth from shadow to shadow. In the thirty-plus years he had lived in this neighborhood he never once ventured out after dark. He tried to walk with a confident gait and stand a little taller than normal in hopes of presenting a more imposing figure, but it failed calm his fears. James felt like a rabbit with a target painted on its side in a shooting gallery.

Zipping up his jacket to block out the cool January evening, he put his hands in his pockets and continued to push his feet forward until he reached the main drag. Turning north, he paused for a moment to watch the sea of cars making slow progress through the evening rush hour. The sidewalks of Central Avenue were alive with activity. Based on his mother's descriptions, he expected to see an apocalyptic wasteland populated only by thugs, drug dealers and homeless vagrants, but quite the opposite was true.

James stood wide-eyed like a child on

Christmas morning, his fear replaced by wonder. There were so many sights, sounds and smells he couldn't possibly take them all in. The sidewalks were filled with workers making their way out of high-rise office buildings, and well dressed couples entering the local restaurants. A light-rail train made its way up the center of the street to the next station where a small group of commuters waited to pack into the already crowded cars. Lights came from everywhere as the pulsing sound of the train wheels on the track resonated through his body.

How could his mother have been so wrong, he thought. The world just beyond his doorstep overflowed with life. Nothing he saw matched the bleak picture Rose painted of the dark, foreboding night-world lurking just a few minutes walk from their narrow street. James felt a little cheated. Had she known about this place all along? Was she trying to hide something from him or just keeping him safe?

He started walking again, trying to absorb everything his senses could handle. Some of his travel articles took Josh to places like this, but he never dreamt he could experience it for himself this close to home.

The heavenly smell as he passed a Mexican restaurant, the buzz of a hundred conversations going on around him, even the aroma coming from the tailpipes of the idling cars waiting at the traffic lights—all of it was intoxicating.

James continued to make his way north, his eyes pointed upward. Each high-rise building he passed was more fascinating than the last. Their faces were covered with hundreds of windows. Some were dark while others were painted with varying levels of light.

He wondered how many people spent their days in each towering structure. His brain did the math while his feet kept pace with the rhythm generated by another passing train.

At one intersection, he crossed to the other side of the street, breaking into a trot when the "Walk" signal suddenly began to flash red as soon as he stepped over the tracks. He passed a large park that included a community garden sectioned off into small plots. The sweet smell of flowers drifted from some areas, the pungent aroma of garlic and onions from others. He passed a school, a church, and then more tall buildings.

James was so overwhelmed by the assault on his senses he lost all track of time. By the time he emerged from his fog over two hours had passed. The traffic had cleared and the once-crowded sidewalks of the central business district gave way to the dark, deserted streets of a residential neighborhood.

The train tracks running down the middle of the street had disappeared, as did the roar of the passing buses. Fear crept back into his mind as he found himself several miles from home with no backup plan.

"Ok, Josh," he muttered under his breath. "What do I do now?"

Josh's voice came back quickly.

Idiot, turn around and walk back the way you came . . . fast!

James spun 180 degrees on his heels and started walking, this time like a man on a mission. His head snapped back and forth, looking for something familiar, but nothing registered with him. He couldn't believe what was happening. Panic gripped his throat as he picked up his pace until he reached a full run. He was lost.

With the sound of his pounding heart beating like a drum in his ears, James almost missed it when the voice of Josh rang out once again.

Don't just run aimlessly. You've written how many survival guides? What's the first rule in every one of 'em? Don't panic! Stop and think, you bonehead. You know this city. You know how it's laid out. Look at the damn street signs and figure out where you are.

Josh was right. James had written a piece on Phoenix and cities like it that were laid out on a grid system. The city of Phoenix had a specific logic to how things were named. The numbered streets ran north-south and the named ones ran east-west. Avenues and drives were west of Central and the streets and places were to the east. Even the address numbers themselves could give him clues as to his direction of travel. The even numbers were on the north and west sides of the streets, while the odds were on the south and east.

James stopped in his tracks and surveyed the area. The first sign he saw was 11th Street and the building he was in front of had an odd numbered address.

"Ok," he mumbled to himself. "I'm a little over a mile east of Central and I'm on the south side of the road. I know I was walking north before, so just head south to the next major street, then west . . . and keep my head down."

Having a plan now, he walked at a more relaxed pace.

You know you could have just looked up. Josh's voice came through with a definite note of sarcasm this time. *Those tall buildings over there? Yeah, they're all on Central Avenue. You walked right by 'em when you were wandering around in your little stupor.*

James shook his head in disgust. He had to agree with his inner voice. How on earth does someone miss a cluster of high-rise buildings?

The temperature was dropping as he made

his way down to Camelback Road and turned back toward the lights of Central Avenue. The cold winter breeze bit at his ears and the tip of his nose. James buried his hands deeper in his pockets and tucked his chin inside his collar of his jacket. When he reached a small pub, he paused where he could feel the warmth radiating from the heaters on the patio. The sounds of laughter and music filtered out to the sidewalk as he tried to get close enough to thaw his chilled flesh without being too obvious.

"It's a whole lot warmer on this side of the fence, son."

James just about jumped out of his skin. As he spun around, he was greeted by a beaming smile attached to a short, stocky woman cleaning one of the outside tables. She looked to be in her late fifties or early sixties. Her voice smiled as much as her face as she spoke with a light Irish accent. "Come on inside an' I'll get ya a hot cup a coffee to wrap yer mitts around."

James replied in a somewhat sheepish voice. "Thank you, but I'm ok. I was just heading home and got a little cold. I'm good now."

"Nonsense!" The little woman stood up straight with her hands on her hips. "Ya get yer skinny little butt in here right now before ya freeze to death!"

That tone of voice was one James

recognized right away. No matter what accent you laid over it, it was the voice of a mother and he knew better than to argue. It was an argument he could never win.

James walked around the corner of the building and, for the first time in his life, stepped through the door of a bar. When he entered the aging structure, the same smiling face and a pair of sparkling green eyes greeted him at the door.

"Go pull yerself up on that stool and I'll get ya that cup a coffee." She waved her hand toward an empty seat at the end of the bar. James followed her instructions like a well trained dog. He watched quietly as she grabbed a heavy oversized mug and headed for the coffee pot. The little woman called back over her shoulder.

"How do ya take it?"

James looked confused. "Excuse me?"

"Yer coffee, how do ya take it?"

"Oh. Just a little cream, I guess"

As his cup of warmth was being prepared, James took in his surroundings. In place of the dimly lit, smoky room he expected to see, there was a bright, colorful Irish themed pub filled with happy patrons and uplifting music. Everyone was engaged in something. There were conversations going on in every corner, people playing darts and billiards, and a particularly rowdy crowd huddled around a large TV watching a soccer game. They would cheer one second and boo the next, cursing and throwing hands in the air.

"Don't pay 'um no mind. Dublin's gittin' their arses handed to 'um. Those boys'll be up and down all night." She placed the big ceramic mug on the bar. "Here ya go son, this otta chase off the shivers."

James reached for his wallet but was quickly reprimanded.

"Don't even think about it. This one's on the house." She extended her hand toward James. "I'm Margie Dugan, but everybody here calls me Mum."

James hesitated for a moment and then reached his own hand across the bar. He shook hers as he spoke. "I'm James . . . James McCarthy."

Margie's eyes lit up even brighter than before and her voice went up an octave. "Oh, my word! A good Irish name! I *knew* there was somethin' special about ya!"

James was more than a little surprised when she scooted around the bar and pulled him off his stool, giving him the tightest hug he had ever experienced. Once he was able to breath again, he managed to get a few words out.

"I'm not that special. I think my father was only half Irish. I'm not really sure."

Stepping back and putting her hands on her hips, Margie narrowed her eyes and spoke in that mother voice again.

"That's good enough fer me. An' don't ya ever let me hear ya say yer not special again!"

James nodded his head and smiled as he slipped back onto his stool and reached for his cup. From the first sip, he knew something wasn't right. He'd had plenty of hot coffee in his time, but this had a different taste and an unfamiliar burn to it . . . a burn that had nothing to do with temperature. His eyes grew wider as he swallowed. He felt the burn spread as the liquid made its way down his throat and reached his stomach.

Margie grinned. "I Irished it up for ya. It'll warm ya from the inside out."

"Thank you . . ." James almost couldn't get the words out. "It seems to be working."

He had read about Irish coffee, but had never experienced it. Truth be told, this was the first time *any* form of alcohol had passed his lips. Rose was very clear about drinking and no doubt would have made him pour the rest out and purge his stomach before the brew worked its evil. But then again, she would have considered it rude to accept a gift and just throw it away. He took another sip. Margie gave him a wink and headed off with a couple more pitchers of beer for the rowdies in the corner.

James continued to survey his new surroundings. The whole place just seemed so alive. A broad swath of humanity appeared to be represented everywhere he turned. There were groups, couples and people drinking alone. He saw men, women, and a few he wasn't really sure about. A large percentage of the patrons spoke with British or Irish accents, but many other countries were also represented.

As he studied the sea of humanity spread out before him, Margie proceeded to fly about the room, feeding and watering everyone, assisted by a rather large red-bearded bartender. She moved so quickly and easily through the crowd that he hadn't even noticed the change in his drink until he turned back toward the bar. He reasoned that Margie must have replaced his empty cup with a full one on one of her passes. He sipped away at the coffee concoction and watched her dance from table to table.

I could get used to this.

Josh echoed a little louder in his head this time. Everything seemed to be echoing a little louder as he got closer to the bottom of his second cup.

Without thinking, James replied out loud. "Yeah, this really looks like your kind of place."

He was startled to hear a female voice answer.

"This is *exactly* my kind of place!"

He quickly spun his stool around and came face to face with the slender young woman now occupying the seat directly to his left. Her jet black hair tumbled down around her shoulders where it met a low-cut, red satin blouse. James felt another wave of warmth wash over him, but it wasn't the booze this time . . . or maybe it was. Either way, getting his eyes to move back up to hers became a problem.

"Um . . . excuse me?" James felt like he was standing on his own tongue.

The woman smiled and leaned closer. "I said this is *exactly* my kind of place."

He swallowed hard and backed off so far he almost fell off his stool. "I'm sorry, I was talking to . . . oh, never mind." James felt himself blushing.

She placed her hand on his knee. "So, what's your name, cutie?"

Before James could answer, Margie popped up and wedged herself between them. The look on her face reminded him of an angry cat protecting its offspring.

Margie spoke through clenched teeth this time. "Ya leave this one alone, Missy! He's not *buyin'* what yer *sellin'!*"

James looked confused. She hadn't tried to sell him anything. She didn't even have any flyers or a business card. What could she possibly have for . . . his brain froze in mid thought as Missy bounced off the seat and sauntered away. His eyes were glued to her tight, black leather pants and high heeled boots.

You know exactly what she's selling.

Josh's words kicked his brain back into gear.

"A nice boy like you don't need a soiled girl like her." Margie was back to the mother voice. "We need ta get ya home before ya get yerself in trouble. Is there anybody I can call fer ya?"

"I can walk. It's only a few miles." James staggered a little as he tried to stand, but plopped right back down on the stool.

Margie smiled, grabbed his arm, and steadied him. "No son, I don't think ya can. Looks like I might'a warmed yer coffee a little too much." She turned her head and yelled back toward the other end of the bar. "Donny! Grab yer coat an' yer keys. This one needs a lift."

James protested. "No, I'm ok. Really."

"Nonsense! My boy'll get ya home safe." Margie grabbed a random business card off the bulletin board next to the bar and scrawled something on the back. "Here's my name an' number. Ya call me tomorrow an' let me know yer ok. Ya understand?"

She slipped the card into his pocket as the sizeable bartender lifted him off the stool and helped him to the door. As the cold night air hit his face, a wobbly James called back to his little Irish savior.

"Thanks, Mom."

Chapter 6

James squeezed his eyes tight as he rolled over, shielding his aching orbs from the morning light streaming in the bedroom window. He twisted under the covers, pulling them up over his head. It felt like his brain lagged two seconds behind his skull whenever he moved. The only time he could remember feeling anything like this was when he contracted a particularly bad stomach flu that kept him in the bathroom and out of school for a few days.

Reluctantly pushing the covers off, he finally emerged from his cocoon appearing more like a ragged moth than a butterfly. Nothing looked right to him as he surveyed his normally organized bedroom. His jeans were in a pile on the floor and one boot stuck out from under the bed. Its mate lay alone in the corner of the room. He saw the toes of his socks peeking out from under his pants, like he had shed all three in one movement. The blue polo shirt was completely missing from the party.

James staggered to the bathroom and flipped the switch on the wall. He quickly flipped it back off again. The diffused light filtering through the curtain on the window was more than enough for his sensitive eyes and didn't seem to hurt as much. He buried his face in the sink, splashing cold water over it with his cupped hands. When he looked in the mirror the man peering back appeared ashen except for the glowing red, bloodshot eyes.

Don't you wish you took that assignment on hangover cures now? Even the imaginary voice of Josh sounded a little louder than normal. James could swear he heard a little chuckle. *If you ask nice, maybe Simon can email you the article.*

Pulling his robe from its hook, James tried to put it on with a minimum of movement. He dragged his feet as he made his way out of the bathroom and down the hallway. He rounded the corner he and tripped on something. He caught himself on the doorway and looked down. Wrapped around his right foot was the blue polo.

One mystery solved, he thought to himself as he kicked free of it. James considered bending over to pick it up, but the idea of his pounding head being lower than the rest of his body didn't really appeal to him. The shirt remained on the floor as he continued toward the kitchen.

After brewing a pot of coffee, *non-Irish*, he filled a large mug and carried it to the table along with a small plate containing two pieces of dry toast. James opted not to butter it, as the thought made him a little queasy. Everything made him a little queasy right now.

Taking a seat, he noticed the worn leather jacket neatly hanging on the back of one the chairs. Every other piece of clothing had ended up on the floor, but not the sacred jacket. Even in his altered state he treated it with respect. It was, after all, the centerpiece of his new image. That image was looking pretty tarnished this morning.

James sipped his coffee and stared off into space, trying to recall the details of the previous evening. He remembered the lights, the sounds and the smells. He remembered getting lost and then finding his way. He remembered the chill of the evening and the warmth of the patio heaters. Everything was clear in his mind . . . right up until his first swallow of that killer coffee. From that point on things got a little hazy. After reaching the bottom of the second cup, it went from hazy to downright foggy.

One thing he did remember clearly was the little Irish woman from the pub. He was pretty sure karma provided her as his guardian angel. She took him in and gave him comfort when he was in need. Her warm hug and cheerful smile made a definite impression on him.

What was her name? Margie? He thought. *Yeah, Margie.*

Margie treated him like she was his own mother. He smiled as he thought to himself. *Well, not his own mother.* His mother never would have ordered him into a bar and gotten him drunk, no matter how cold it was. On the plus side, she made her son drive him home. She also saved him from the clutches of a young woman he assumed was likely a prostitute.

Josh's voice came through very suggestive this time. *She called her Missy.*

James started getting that warm feeling again as he recalled the image of her dancing away in those tight leather pants.

How long do you think it took her to stretch those things over that ass? Josh taunted. *Better yet, how long do think it would take to get 'em off?*

James felt himself blushing at the thought. He had never been approached by a woman like her before. In fact, he had never been approached by *any* woman before. When her hand touched his leg, something deep inside of him came alive. The same feelings he managed to push down and bury in his high school years had awakened and Josh was eating it up.

James thought his mother might have been wrong about some things, but in this case she may have been right on the money. Maybe alcohol and women of questionable morals *do* go hand in hand. Josh interjected his opinion on the subject.

I think we might need to do a little more research on that one!

Trying to refocus himself, James took a bite of the toast and raised the cup to his lips again. His memory started to clear up a little as the coffee worked its magic with the help of a couple aspirin. The memory of Margie slipping the card in his jacket as Donny escorted him out the door came into focus.

"Oh man," he whined. "I'm supposed to call and let her know I'm ok . . . even if I'm not."

Leaning over and fishing around in the coat pocket, James produced a fading business card. Printed across the face in large letters was 'Rose Tattoo,' underneath it the words 'Ken Murphy - Artist and Manager.' He flipped the card over and read the name scrawled above the phone number on the back. 'Margie Dugan - AKA Mum.'

He deposited his dishes in the sink and returned to the table, grabbing the cordless phone out of its cradle as he passed. As he dialed the number, he could feel his nerves kicking in. He was sure Margie had dealt with her fair share of drunken patrons over the years, so would she even remember him?

"Good morning!" The happy voice on the other end of the line sounded almost like singing. "This is Margie."

"H-hi," James stuttered a little. "Um, we

met last night and . . ."

Margie's voice got even higher as she cut him off. "Mr. McCarthy, is that you? I was gettin' a little worried. Donny said ya made it in the door last night, but he couldn't say if ya made it all the way to the bed."

James pulled the phone away from his ear a few inches as her voice pierced his brain. "Yeah, I made it ok," he said at a low volume. "I just wanted to thank you for helping me out last night. Can you thank your son for me too? I really don't remember much about the drive home."

Margie laughed. "Sorry, Jimmy boy. That was my fault, and don't worry, I'll bet ya didn't miss a thing. My Donny ain't much of a talker 'til he gets to know ya, then ya can't shut 'im up!"

"It's ok." James was trying to speak as soft as he could and still be heard. "It wasn't entirely your fault. I should have told you I'm not much of a drinker."

Margie giggled. "No, I'd say yer not. Ya went down pretty fast last night. Ya sound a little rough this morning as well. Have ya got someone there to take care of ya?"

"No." He started to choke on his words. "My mother passed away a few months ago, so I live alone now, but I'll be ok . . . really."

The other end of the phone went silent.

When Margie finally spoke, her voice sounded soft and warm. "Why don't ya come on over to the pub an' we'll see if we can't fix ya up."

James hesitated. "I don't know. I really don't feel like . . ."

Margie interrupted him. "Don't worry, no hair of the dog cures in this house. Ya get yerself cleaned up an' come see me. I've got just the thing to set ya right again."

"Alright." In one evening James had already learned not to argue with her. "Thank you again, Mrs. Dugan."

"Mrs. Dugan was my mother-in-law." Margie was still speaking in that soft tone, "Yer one of *my* boys now. Ya just call me Mum."

James hung up the phone and headed back down the hall toward the bathroom, stepping over the blue shirt one more time. He really wasn't looking forward to going out in the bright sunlight today, but he didn't feel like he had much of a choice either. Margie insisted and he relented, so that was that. Once James gave his word, he never went back on it. To be honest, he also caved kind of quickly because he liked the idea that someone else actually cared about him.

As he showered and dressed, he thought about what life might have been like growing up under the care of Margie instead of his own strict, protective, and emotionally distant mother. What would he have done differently? Who might he have become?

Josh was quick to answer once again. *You would have become me.*

James was a little annoyed at the thought. "Right, that's just the headache talking."

No, Josh insisted. *You would have turned out just like me. I'm everything you wanted but were afraid to go after, or at least your mother was afraid for you to go after. Damn it, you created me to do what you couldn't!*

James had no counterpoint for that statement. He couldn't argue with the truth. As he finished getting dressed, Josh continued his diatribe.

Everything I am came from somewhere inside of you. It's all in your crazy, repressed brain just waiting to dig its way out. Sure, Margie might have been responsible for the first swallow last night, but who finished those drinks? That was me! Who do you think picked out those jeans and boots . . . and your precious damn jacket? It sure as hell wasn't the guy who sits in front of that computer screen all day and fantasizes about being somewhere else.

James slipped on the jacket and picked up his keys as he opened the door. He squinted and lowered his head as the bright light of day hit his face.

"Alright, Josh," James said out loud." If you're so smart, why did you stop me from buying the sunglasses?"

Chapter 7

Driving through downtown Phoenix, James noted it looked much the same as it did on any other day. The magical night world he experienced gave way to the usual dirty streets, honking cars, and forest of tall buildings blocking out the hazy sky. Even the people milling around the light rail stations on Central seemed less interesting in the bright light of day. He couldn't believe this was the same city that had so captivated him just a few hours earlier.

He was also surprised to find himself heading to a bar . . . and at eleven o'clock in the morning. It felt more like something Josh would do. James was convinced if his mother had still been alive, the events of the last twenty-four hours would surely have killed her. In addition to that Margie, another mother, waited for him at the end of this drive—waiting to fix what she had broken the previous night.

James looked forward to seeing Margie again, but felt a little guilty about it. He wasn't looking to replace his mother and didn't want to disrespect her, but the thought of a warm hug and a kind word from his *new* mom had already dulled the pain in his head. He didn't understand how he could have such an immediate connection with another person, but what he really didn't get was how anyone could have that connection with him at all.

You're not that bad, Josh interjected. *Besides, the way you were dressed last night you looked a little like me. I'm sure that's what she was responding to.*

James frowned. "Yeah, right. I think it was because I looked so pathetic standing out there on the street trying to get warm."

Ah, lost puppy syndrome. He was almost sure he heard that chuckle in Josh's voice again. *What about that other woman? What do you think she was responding to? If it was the lost puppy thing, I'd make damn sure I kept that arrow in my quiver.*

"I think it's more likely she saw a drunk talking to himself and thought, 'wow, an easy target.'"

Josh was undeterred. *Hey, whatever works.*

As James turned the car into the parking lot of Dugan's Public House his nerves started to kick in again. He didn't know whether to be excited or scared. Mostly he wanted the hangover to be done. He had no idea what Margie had in store for him, but he figured she couldn't make it any worse. Even if her cure made him throw up, he felt like it would be a step in the right direction.

Walking through the door, James was surprised to see the pub full of people. He hadn't expected to encounter a crowd in a bar this early on a weekday, but very few tables were empty. The lighting had been turned up brighter and the music played lower than the night before. The rowdy footballers and pitchers of beer had been replaced by people dressed for business with glasses of soda and iced tea. Daylight had converted the raucous pub into a respectable restaurant.

James looked around for a familiar face. Donny was behind the bar restocking bottles and wiping down the back counter. There were several stools empty, so James headed for one. He really didn't know Donny, but the man had already seen him at his most vulnerable and didn't rob him blind or hurt him, so he figured he'd at least be safe there. As he slid onto the stool, Donny turned around. The big redheaded bartender grinned from ear to ear. He also spoke with an Irish accent, though not as thick as his mother's.

"Look what the cat dragged in. Ya look a little rough around the edges. Did ya make it past the couch last night? Mom was a little worried about ya."

"Yeah," James answered sheepishly. "I woke up in bed this morning, but I don't really remember how I got there. Thanks for me getting home. I owe you one."

Donny shook his head. "No, that one was

on the house. I think mother dear must of dipped into her private stock for ya last night. That stuff'll take the finish off the bar if ya spill it."

James tried to manage a smile, but it hurt. "That coffee did hit me a little hard. I've never had anything like that before. I'm not really much of a drinker."

The sarcasm in Donny's voice was obvious. "No kiddin'? I never would'a guessed." He gave a little laugh. "Good Irish whiskey ain't for beginners, Jimmy. Next time, ya come 'n see me first. We'll put the training wheels on and maybe start ya with a little rum in something fruity."

James glared at Donny from under his furrowed brow and spoke in a tone more likely to come out of Josh's mouth. "Yeah, thanks… thanks a lot."

Donny grinned and saluted before turning back to his work. Margie emerged from the kitchen. Her face lit up when she spotted her newest son planted in the same seat he had occupied the previous evening. James hadn't even realized that fact until it was too late.

"Returned to the scene of the crime, I see." Margie was bearing down on him fast, arms spread for another one of those giant hugs. "How's the head?"

He was pretty sure she already knew the

answer to that question. "A little tender, but tolerable," he volunteered as she squeezed the air out of him.

Margie felt his forehead and rubbed his cheek. "Let's see what we can do to fix that." She turned her head and called out. "Donny! Tell Miguel ta bring out a bowl of the good stuff!"

As Donny stuck his head in the kitchen, James got a little worried. Wasn't the 'good stuff' responsible for causing this hangover to begin with? A few moments later a short, gray haired Hispanic man emerged from the kitchen carrying a steaming bowl of what appeared to be some kind of soup and placed it on the bar in front of James.

The smell rising from the concoction was intoxicating. It was spicy with a hint of citrus and a lot of other things James couldn't even start to identify. On the plate next to it was a little foil packet containing a warm flour tortilla folded neatly into quarters. James was confused.

"Isn't this an Irish bar? This smells like Mexican food."

Margie laughed as she handed him a big spoon. "Irish hangover cures mostly involve stayin' drunk," she said with a wink. "This is menudo, and there's no better medicine for the bottle flu. It's not on the menu, but Miguel always keeps a little pot of it warm in the kitchen just for this kind of emergency His wife makes it, and you'll never find better. If this don't fix ya up, nothin' will."

James remembered coming across the supposed miracle cure somewhere in his research for a write up on local cuisine. He couldn't remember everything in the wonder soup, but he did recall the main ingredient — tripe, the lining of a cow's stomach. He winced as he turned his head, looking Margie square in the eyes.

"Cow stomach is supposed to make me feel better?" As the bile crept up in his throat he could hear Josh cackling in his head.

"Yes." Margie used the mother voice again. "It's gonna make ya feel better. Ya just get that spoon movin' and you'll be back on yer feet in no time."

"Ya better listen to her," Donny called back over his shoulder, "Yer gonna find out she's always right, even when she's not."

In one motion Margie spun on her heels and smacked Donny in the back of the head as she admonished him. "Ya watch yer mouth, boy!" The big man just laughed it off and headed into the kitchen. Margie turned back toward James. "Eat up, son."

He leaned over and quickly plunged the spoon into the bowl. Not wanting to receive the same treatment as Donny, he kept one eye on Margie as the first mouthful passed his lips. By the time the warm liquid hit his tongue, he could already feel the spices starting to penetrate his sinus cavity. With the second spoonful, the warmth spread down his throat and into his chest. James could not believe the feeling. By the time he reached the bottom of the bowl most of his symptoms were already beginning to fade.

He looked up from the empty bowl to find Margie had disappeared. She had been replaced by Donny, who slid a glass in front of him. Even Josh sounded a little scared this time.

Oh lord! What do you think is in that? Is the big guy trying to get us drunk again?

Donny must have seen the look of horror on James' face.

"Don't worry," Donny reassured as he placed a couple of ibuprofen tablets on the bar next to the drink. "It's just iced tea with a little mint. You need to get rehydrated to kill the headache. The mint helps to calm your belly."

"Thanks." James and Josh both breathed a sigh of relief as he swallowed the pills. "But I've just got to ask. Why are you guys being so nice to me? I mean, you don't really know me. I could be an axe murderer for all you know."

Donny let out a laugh so loud everyone in the bar stopped what they were doing for a moment and looked up. He waved at the crowd then pointed back down at James.

"First off, I doubt those skinny little arms could even pick up an axe. Second, Mom likes you and while she might be wrong about some things, and don't you ever tell her I said that, she's never wrong about people."

"I guess that's what I don't get." James rubbed his neck as he shook his head. "She saw me for a few seconds last night and that was it. All of the sudden it's like we've known each other for years. And it's not just her; I'm doing the same thing. When she says jump, I'm not even hesitating to ask how high."

"Well," Donny stroked his beard and looked pensive. "Let me give this one a shot before you ask her. You wandered up here lookin' pretty pathetic last night, damn near jumpin' that fence to get warm. That bit right there probably kicked her motherly instincts into overdrive. The pale face could a told her you don't get out much, and the fact you're not carryin' a cell phone says you got no one to call. That means you probably live alone and don't have any friends to speak of.

"Everybody needs somebody, an' she's more than happy to be that somebody. She thinks it's her callin'."

James looked shocked. "Wow, you're

good."

"No." Donny smiled. "I just know my mother. You better be savin' her number and keepin' it close to your heart. She's gonna be checkin' up on you pretty regular now that she knows your mother has passed."

"I'd do that," James said as he shifted on the stool, "but you were right. I don't even own a cell phone. I've never really had a need for one. You were on the money when you said I don't have anyone to call."

"Well, you do now."

Donny dug behind the bar and came up with a well worn magazine. He stuck his thumb into the gap at a dog-eared page and flipped it open in front of James.

"Might as well read the reviews on the latest smart phones 'cause I have a feelin' you'll be gettin' one very soon. This guy seems to know what he's talkin' about. I read his stuff all the time."

James looked down at the magazine on the bar and just about choked. The author of the article was . . . Josh McDaniel.

"You read Josh's articles? Really?"

Donny looked a little surprised. "Yeah, you know about him?"

James smiled. "I guess you could say that.

We're actually pretty close."

"Really?" Donny looked confused. "I thought you said you didn't have any friends."

"Well," James couldn't wipe the smile off his face, "I wouldn't exactly call us friends. I help him, he helps me. It's a complicated relationship."

"Oh," Donny nodded. "So you guys work together?"

James nodded back in agreement. "Yup, I do all the work, and he gets all the credit."

"Damn." Donny looked disappointed. "I really thought the guy was smart. I've bought a lot a stuff on his word an' it all seems to be good. My wife even uses his travel guides to plan our vacations. So, you say you're the brains behind him, eh? What are you, his research assistant or his editor?"

"More like ghost writer."

James hated to burst the big guy's bubble, but he just couldn't bite his tongue any longer.

"I know we just met, but for some reason I already feel like I can trust you. You're kind of supposed to be my big brother now, right? Can you to keep a secret? You have to promise not to tell anyone, not even your mother."

Donny leaned in, shifting his eyes from side to side like a spy in some old black and white movie.

"You got my word, Bro."

James leaned in as well and spoke in a whisper. "I *am* Josh McDaniel."

Chapter 8

James sat down at his desk and fumbled with the new piece of technology in his hands. Just as Donny had predicted, Margie insisted he get a cell phone and keep it with him at all times. His new brother almost had a stroke trying to contain his reaction when she pushed the same article in front of him and began running on about the wisdom of its author. Donny even retreated to the kitchen, banging pots and pans around in an unsuccessful attempt to cover his hysterical laughter.

Judging by Donny's reaction, James wasn't even sure that he believed the confession but, true to his word, he hadn't spilled the beans about the real identity of Josh McDaniel. James figured he might as well have claimed to be Superman. No doubt the reaction would have been the same, considering how Donny felt about the wise and all-knowing journalist he placed up on that pedestal. None the less, a bond seemed to have been forged between the two and sealed with the secret.

As James continued to explore the new smart phone, he looked at his contact list. He couldn't help but feel pathetic. There were only two entries—Margie and Donny. He added Simon's phone number and email address just to make himself feel better, but he had to admit it was still pretty sad. How could he have lived on this earth for thirty-one years and have only one business associate and two people he had just met to show for it?

Still, he thought, his two new acquaintances were something special. He had gone from being an only child and totally alone to having a family of sorts in the space of only a couple of days. Somehow, he had gained a loving little fireball of a mother figure and a happy, wisecracking pseudo-brother, and more family waited in the wings. He had yet to meet Donny's wife and Margie's younger son, Will.

Josh had something to say about his contact list as well.

Where are all the single women? We need to get out there and circulate a little. Time to let all the ladies know we're on the market!

"Great," James sighed. "And just how do you propose I do that? I don't even know where to meet women, and even if I did, what would I say? They might see a little of Josh because of the clothes, but when I open my mouth it's still going to be James that comes out."

You already know the where," Josh replied. *You just need to go when your new mom isn't around to run interference. As for the how, well you just have a couple of those fruity drinks Donny mentioned and I'll take over from there.*

James frowned. "That's exactly what I'm afraid of . . ."

James thought another encounter with alcohol might remove his inhibitions enough to interact with the women at the pub, but at the same time he feared it would also allow the persona of Josh a little *too* much freedom. He knew he needed Josh's swagger, but not an over abundance of it. Control had to be the word of the day. He needed to find a way to let Josh out to play while keeping him on a short leash.

James reasoned moderation was going to be his best approach. He did a quick internet search to try and determine what he should drink and how much. The general rule of thumb seemed to be one drink per hour according to most sources, just enough to lower his inhibitions, but not enough to make him totally hand the reins over to Josh. Stick to something with a lower alcohol content and sip. No shooting or chugging allowed.

With that detail of his plan out of the way, James moved on the next roadblock—Margie. A quick text exchange with Donny cleared the path. Margie volunteered a couple evenings a month at a local hospital, reading fairytales and bedtime stories to the children and, as luck would have it, she was filling in for another reader that night. The pub would be in Donny's hands and mother-free until at least ten o'clock.

"No more excuses," he declared. "Tonight's the night."

The rest of the day flew by as James tried to catch up on his work. The previous day's hangover had brought production to a screeching halt and for the first time in his life, James needed to push to make a deadline. His progress was also being hampered by nerves. As the countdown clock to the launch of his social life wound down, he found it harder and harder to focus. With only five minutes to spare, he sent the last article to Simon and shut his computer down, closing up shop for the weekend.

James didn't normally take weekends off. His days usually blended one into the other with no downtime. It wasn't about the money. His mother's life insurance left him with a substantial nest egg, and he owed nothing on the house or car. For him, the work meant an escape from boredom and the chance to live through the exploits of his alter ego. This Friday was different. James wanted to leave his computer behind and step into the "real world" for some exploits of his own.

Making his way through the rush hour traffic, he was both excited and anxious at the same time. The whole idea of meeting and talking to members of the opposite sex played on his numerous insecurities. The fact he would be taking the plunge in what was fast becoming a familiar watering hole gave him some comfort. He did carry some guilt about feeling at home in a bar. Rose would not have approved in any way, shape, or form. As much as he loved his late mother, he didn't let that stop him from turning into the parking lot.

The regular Friday evening crowd was beginning to filter in as James walked through the door of Dugan's. He worked his way through the crowd and headed toward the bar where he was greeted by Miguel, who happily bussed the tables as he whistled along with the music that filled the air.

"Señor James!" Miguel seemed genuinely happy to see him. "How are you feeling today?"

James had to laugh as he answered. "Much better, thank you. I feel like my head's back on my shoulders where it belongs. Thanks for the soup. I'm pretty sure it saved my life."

Miguel chuckled. "The first hangover is always the worst, but your eyes look a better color today. You go easy tonight my friend, ok?"

"Ok." James nodded and shook the man's hand. "I promise."

With that the two men parted and James

continued on to what had become his usual stool at the end of the bar. Once again Donny's smiling face greeted him.

"Back for more punishment?"

James nodded. "Yeah, figured I might as well go for round two, but I'm taking it a little easier this time. What have you got that won't make me regret my decision?"

"Let's see what we can do." As he spoke, Donny's hands started moving behind the bar like a conductor in front of an orchestra. "You know mom's not here tonight, right? Didn't I tell ya she's at the hospital with the kids?"

"Yeah, I know," James admitted. "I was kind of hoping to maybe do some socializing tonight and . . . "

Donny held up a hand.

"Say no more!" He was grinning from ear to ear now. "When the cat's away, the mice will play. Mum does have a tendency to scare the ladies off if she thinks they're not good enough for ya . . . and in her estimation, *no one* will be good enough for ya. I never even told her I was dating Jen 'til we were damn near married!"

James looked worried. "How did she take the news when you finally told her?"

"Blew her stack!" Donny stood tall and actually sounded proud of it. "Didn't talk to me for a week."

"So, she didn't like your choice for a wife, huh?"

"Loved her!" Donny replied with a smile. "I came home and found the two of 'em drunk, sitting at the kitchen table telling stories and making fun of my childhood pictures. They've been thick as thieves ever since."

Donny laid a napkin on the bar and placed a glass on it. The drink appeared to be a clear liquid on ice, with lime and some muddled mint.

"Mojito!" He declared as he pushed it toward James. "I went easy on the rum this time. We'll see how you do before we go any stronger."

James reached for wallet, but like his mother had done before, Donny stopped him.

"Your money's no good in here. Yer family now Jimmy, you drink for free."

"Family . . ." James looked up at Donny. "I don't even know what that really means."

Donny smiled. "It means you got people, ones you can *really* count on. Family is the tree ya sprung from, or in your case the one you got grafted to."

"So tell me about your family." James looked around at all of the Irish sports memorabilia covering the walls. "Tell me about this place. Did your parents build it?"

"Not my parents, my Uncle Tommy." Donny pointed at one of soccer jerseys framed above the bar. "He played for the national team. When they came here to play a tournament, he fell in love with a woman and decided to stay. He opened this place to make a living and try to bring a little of the old country with him."

"So how did your parents end up here?" James inquired.

Donny stroked his beard and tried to recall the tale.

"Well, we lived on the family farm outside of Galway. I was just a lad of about four, when we left. Willy hadn't even been born yet. I guess Papa wasn't cut out to be a farmer, and Uncle Tommy got pretty homesick after his break-up. The two of 'em worked out some kinda trade. Uncle Tommy went back to the land, and we ended up here."

James wasn't sure if he should ask his next question, but he did anyway. "Where is your father?"

Donny choked up as he answered.

"He . . . he got killed during a robbery a few years back. Some bloke crazy on meth waited for him to close up then jumped him on the way to the car. Papa give him the money without a fight, but the bastard shot him anyway. Nobody closes up alone anymore. Miguel won't hear of it. He don't leave here 'til he walks the last soul out. Even comes in at closing time on the nights he don't work. Papa was his best friend. It hurt him bad. He swore on Papa's grave he'd make sure nothin' like that happened here again."

"I'm sorry." James hung his head. "I shouldn't have asked. It's really none of my business."

"It's your family now too, Jimmy." Donny reached over the bar and put a hand on his shoulder. "You got a right to know the history. Now let's lighten the mood and get back to what you come in here for."

"That sounds like a good idea." James picked up his drink and eyeballed it. "Do you think this will help me talk to women? I've never been any good at it. Okay, I've never really done it."

Donny smiled. "Alcohol is a fine social lubricant when applied properly, but at some point it's all up to you."

"Well then," James lifted the glass and looked at Donny. "Here's to social lubricants." And with that, he took a sip.

A smile came across his face. He found the drink surprisingly refreshing and didn't taste the alcohol at all. The concoction went down easier than he expected—the complete opposite of

Margie's coffee. He raised the glass and took another sip.

"Pace yourself," Donny warned. "It's gonna be a long night. Those things are *real* easy to drink. You don't want 'em sneaking up on ya."

"Right." James nodded and set the drink back down on the bar. "The goal is to loosen up a little, not to lose control."

"Exactly." Donny leaned in and lowered his voice. "So, you lookin' for a relationship or just wanna have some fun?"

James was dumbfounded. "I . . . I don't know. I've never done this before."

"Right then." Donny looked amused. "Fun it is!"

The big man straightened up and started surveying the room. "Looks like there might be some potential in here tonight. The rebroadcast of the Manchester United game is gonna start in about twenty minutes. Once that kicks off most of these guys wouldn't notice Lady Godiva ridin' through the place. That should thin out the competition a bit."

James caught himself laughing. "You sound like you've done this before . . . a lot!"

Donny gave him a wink. "Just 'cause I'm married don't mean I can't be a good wingman. It's a bartender's sworn duty and besides, mother dear said to help you out any way I can. The way I see it, I'm just followin' orders."

"Ok, Wingman." James was already starting to sound more like Josh as the alcohol kicked in. "What's my first move?"

Donny thought for a second. "Well, I'd say your first move is to stop introducing yourself as James—sounds too stuffy. You need to be Jim or Jimmy. Yeah, that's it! You're now *Jimmy McCarthy*."

"Ok," James responded. "But I don't know how that's supposed to help me talk to women."

Donny shrugged his shoulders. "Couldn't hurt, right?"

James turned his stool toward the crowd, picking up his drink and sipping it slowly as Donny went back to work. There were quite a few women spread around the room. Many of them appeared to be with other men, but quite a few were unencumbered. Some small groups were clustered around tables, and a handful of potential candidates sat at the other end of the bar.

Just as Donny predicted, the start of the game changed the dynamic of the pub completely. A good percentage of the men who had been milling about were now totally focused on the screen in the corner. Some of the women were also watching, but not a great number of them. Most had been abandoned by their potential suitors and were now turning their attentions elsewhere.

Over to one side of the room next to the dart board, James noticed two young women sitting at one of the high-top tables. The one facing him looked somewhat plain with her straight brown hair and thick glasses. She was dressed conservatively, like she had just come from a long day at the office. On the other side of the table, he saw a slimmer, dark haired woman sitting with her back toward him. She had on tight jeans and a white t-shirt that appeared to be about two sizes too small.

Hey bonehead! The rum was starting to fuel Josh up. *I think office girl just smiled at you. Get over there and introduce yourself!*

"I can't," James protested in his head. "She's with that other girl."

Oh, so the hot one's scaring you off? Josh chided. *Don't worry about her. She's out of your league anyway. You're new at this. It's ok to go for the low hanging fruit.*

James finished off his drink and summoned every bit of courage he could muster. As he began to lift himself off the stool, the dark haired girl turned her head. When he recognized the profile, he panicked.

"Oh no, that's Missy!"

Spinning back around on the stool, James

put his elbows on the bar and buried his chin in his chest as Donny walked up with another drink.

"Yeah, that's Missy alright. You gonna go talk to her?"

"*No!*" James was visibly shaken. "She a prostitute, isn't she?"

Donny let out a huge laugh. "Where in the hell did you get that idea?"

He looked up at Donny, who was still trying to recover his composure. "From your mom! She said Missy was selling it the other night. I just assumed she meant she was selling, you know… *it!*"

"Oh, *hell* no," Donny replied, trying not to laugh again. "If that girl's selling it, she's not makin' any money. It's more like she's trading it for two drinks and a burger. I'm not surprised Mom has a pretty low opinion of her. She don't go home alone very often, but she's no hooker. If you ask me, she's got daddy issues or somethin'. I think she's punishin' her parents."

"Well that's a relief," James sighed. "But I still don't think I'm ready to talk to her."

"Well, you better get yourself ready." Donny was beaming. "She's at your six o'clock and closin' in fast!"

Chapter 9

James took a huge swallow from the new glass Donny had provided. He had somewhat prepared himself to talk to the plain-Jane looking woman on the other side of the table, but Missy? She played in a different league. Missy was attractive, uninhibited, and *very* experienced. He imagined she had probably been approached by every unattached male in the bar at some point. Odds were she had gone home with a good number of them as well. So, why had she set her sights on him, he wondered. What could he possibly have to offer that would interest a woman like her?

You're fresh meat, Josh answered. *Unexplored territory.*

Maybe that was it, James thought. He was the new prey that had wandered into her familiar hunting ground. That thought didn't help at all. James still had no idea what to say. Panic started taking over his brain as Missy drew closer.

"Josh, don't fail me now!" He thought to himself.

James took one more drink and spun his stool around, coming face to face with his would-be predator.

"Well, look who's back," Missy purred. "I

never did get your name the other night."

James choked on his words.

"Ja..." He flashed a quick side glance at Donny. "Um . . . Jimmy, my name is Jimmy McCarthy."

He extended his hand to shake hers. She grabbed it, pulling him close and giving him a quick kiss on the cheek as she jumped onto the adjacent stool. "I'm Melissa, but everybody calls me Missy," she said still clutching his hand.

"And *everybody* calls her," Donny was quick to interject.

Missy shot him a dirty look and then turned back to James. "You must be new around here. I would have remembered *that* face."

"Um . . . yeah," James stammered. "I mean no. I've lived in Phoenix all my life, I've just never been in here before . . . well, before the other night anyway."

"Really?" Missy kind of screwed up one side of her face. "The way Margie came out swinging the other night I thought maybe you were one of Donny's cousins visiting from out of town or something. She chased me off like you were blood."

James started to open his mouth to speak, but Donny beat him to it.

"I'd be lucky to have him as a cousin. This

one's smart—smarter than you and me put together." Donny gave him a wink. "I love him like a brother. Why, he's like the genius little brother I never had."

James wasn't sure what to say. He decided he should just shut up and let his wingman work.

Missy shook her head. "You big idiot, you *have* a little brother."

"Yeah." Donny smiled, leaning in and lowering his voice "But he ain't no genius."

"Oh, like you're one to talk." She turned her nose up at Donny. "Think you're smart enough to make me a rum and coke?"

"Sure." He smiled and shrugged his shoulders. "You just tell me what's in one and I'll be happy to make it."

With that, the big man spun on his heels and headed to the other end of the bar, leaving James to fend for himself.

Missy turned her attention back to James, who by now felt a little more confident, though he really wasn't sure why. Maybe it was the build up Donny had given him, or it could have been the alcohol pumping through his veins. Either way his fear melted enough to at least allow him to talk to her without tripping over his own tongue.

"Donny may have exaggerated a little bit. I'm not really a genius, but I do ok." James surprised himself as he spoke in a fairly normal tone. Josh was definitely starting to take over and drive the conversation. "So you seem to know this place pretty well. Are you from around here, too?"

"I'm in here a lot. I only live a few blocks away." She shifted in her seat. "But we're not talking about me right now. Tell me why Donny thinks you're such a genius. Are you some kind of scientist or something?"

James laughed out loud. "Oh, God no! I'm just a writer. I do research, sum up the results and then sell the articles to magazines and websites."

"Nice, so you're slumming it." She looked straight at Donny, who had just returned with her drink. "Most of the guys in this place can't even read a magazine, let alone write for one. Why the hell would you want to hang out in here?"

"You want the truth?" He looked at Donny, as if waiting for a sign of approval. "I was out for a walk the other night and I got cold. Margie made me come in to get warmed up, and then she kind of adopted me."

Donny chimed in. "A fine addition to the family, don't you think?"

Missy was quick to fire back. "Certainly raises the average IQ. Kind of makes up for you, right?"

"I love you too, lady." And with that Donny

sarcastically blew her a kiss and headed toward the customers at the other end of the bar.

"So," Missy focused her attention back on James. "You and Donny seem to have hit it off."

James nodded in agreement. "Yes, it actually feels a little strange though. I kind of grew up alone . . . well, except for my mother. Anyway, it feels kind of weird having a sort of big brother. Don't get me wrong, I like having someone looking out for me, it's just that I've never had that before. I guess I haven't gotten used to it yet."

"Yeah." She smiled as she glanced in Donny's direction. "He's a big goof and a total pain in the ass, but I guess he's ok. I just give him shit because I can, and he doesn't have any problem giving it right back."

"I wish I could be a little more like him." James looked somewhat pensive. "I mean, he has no problem talking to anybody. I can barely open my mouth around someone I don't know."

Missy spoke in a soft, sexy voice as she looked James directly in the eye. "You seem to be doing just fine right now."

James fumbled nervously for his glass and held it up. "Social lubricant!"

"You *have* been talking to Donny," Missy giggled. "That's his solution for... well, come to think of it, that's his solution to just about everything."

James couldn't help but smile. "I guess that's what makes him a good bartender."

"Somebody mention my name?" Donny's timing couldn't have been better if he'd planned it. "You kids getting' along ok over here? Is everybody playin' nice?"

"I was just telling Jimmy what a loser you are," she replied with a smirk.

Donny smiled. "Two crazy kids like yourselves and the only subject you can come up with is me? Don't get me wrong, I'm flattered and all but you gotta have better things to discuss. Jimmy, did you tell her your secret?"

"Um . . . no. I have a secret?" He wasn't sure where Donny was going with this one.

"You know." Donny winked "About that other guy you work with? She's a big fan. Even has a couple of them books."

Missy perked up. "What other guy? I've got lots of books."

"Our boy here is connected." Donny stood straight and proud as he spoke. "You know them travel books you're always dreamin' in? Well, Jimmy here is *really* close to that Josh guy that writes 'em."

"You know Josh McDaniel?" Missy almost jumped out of her seat.

"Well . . . yeah." James could feel Josh swelling up inside his head. "We work together."

"Oh, don't be shy Jimmy boy." Donny shifted into full wingman mode again as he turned his attention to Missy. "If it wasn't for this guy, there wouldn't even *be* a Josh McDaniel. The man can't make a move without our boy here."

Missy grabbed James' arm and shook him as she ran on excitedly.

"Is he married? I'll bet he's single! He can't do all of that traveling and be married. What does he look like? Can you introduce me?"

James looked at Donny. His wingman wore a grin that stretched from ear to ear. The man almost couldn't contain himself as he waited to see how James would talk his way around this one. When she finally took a breath, words started falling out of James' mouth. He was clearly lubricated.

"I'm afraid he's out of the country right now." He couldn't believe how easily the lie was forming as he stared into the crystal blue eyes now locked on to his. "He may not be back for a few weeks. Um, he's doing research . . . in Peru. No cell service or internet in the mountains, so I don't really know when I'll hear from him."

Missy was undeterred. "So, is he married? Does he have a girlfriend?"

"He's single," he replied. "But he's kind of a cad. He just uses women and then moves on. He'll never commit to one, it's just not who he is. He's a real narcissist—only loves himself."

"Wow . . ." Missy seemed a little disillusioned. "He sounds so cool when he writes about people and places. I mean, he can't be that bad. Is he really that bad?"

"Oh, worse . . . much worse." James was starting to enjoy trashing Josh's character. "He also drinks way too much . . . and he's not allowed back in Mexico, but I can't really talk about that—Judge's orders. As for the writing, well, I do most of that. He travels and I write about it. That's kind of our arrangement."

"Are you serious?" Missy frowned, the excitement completely gone from her voice. "Man that *really* sucks. He seemed like such a cool guy. I mean, I would have probably gone home with him in a heartbeat."

"Well," Donny cocked his head in James' direction as he spoke. "You could still go home with the guy that *really* writes that stuff."

Missy looked straight into James' eyes again. "Did you really . . . I mean *really* write those books?"

"Yeah." James was more subdued now as he nodded. He felt some guilt about lying to her starting to settle in. "I write the articles and the books, but Josh's name goes on them."

"Why?" She seemed to genuinely want to know the answer—the real answer.

James squirmed on his stool as he pondered how much he should tell. "It's kind of a long story. Are you sure you want to hear it?"

"Yeah." She took his hand and stroked it gently as she spoke. "I don't know why, but I think I actually do."

Donny sighed and shook his head as he quickly palmed the condom he planned to secretly slip to James.

"Gettin' all serious on me, eh? Looks like we're gonna be here a while. Why don't you two go park yourselves at that table in the corner where you can have a little more privacy." He motioned toward a booth at the back of the room. "I'll get you some food to soak up the booze."

Missy held tightly to James' hand as the pair made their way through the crowded bar. For some reason, the normally brash and confident young woman appeared nervous. Her usual "don't tell me your sad story and I won't tell you mine" approach to dealing with the opposite sex looked to be going out the window. Somehow the man now slipping into the secluded booth with her was different. He didn't quite fit into her world, yet she found herself wanting to know more about him, and that scared her.

James was surprised to discover he felt a little *less* uncomfortable. He no longer thought about how Josh would handle the situation; in fact, he wasn't thinking about Josh at all. The original plan of gaining some experience with women took a backseat to learning more about *this* woman—the one still gripping his hand tight. Josh probably would have used the information to find her weak points and seduce her, but James found himself truly interested in learning her story.

The two sat staring at each other for what seemed like an eternity. Missy broke the silence as she finally released his hand.

"So, what's the story with you and Josh McDaniel? From the way you talk, I'm guessing you don't like him very much."

"It's kind of complicated," James replied as he folded his arms on the table. "Can I tell you a secret? You might hate me . . . and I wouldn't blame you."

Missy looked worried. "That sounds a little ominous, but I don't even know you, so how can I hate you?"

"Ok, I'll give you the real story." James got a little uncomfortable again. "You have to promise not to tell anyone. Only two other people know this, my editor and Donny . . . and I'm not sure Donny really believes me."

"Ok, I promise." Missy leaned in closer. "So, tell me already!"

James took a deep breath. "Josh McDaniel doesn't really exist. He's just a character I created so no one would know *I* wrote those articles."

"What?" Missy's eyes widened. "You're kidding me, right? The traveling, the women . . . you want me to believe you did all that? I'm not buying it."

"No." James explained. "I didn't do *any* of those things. Nobody did, that's the point. I'm supposed to be some kind of expert on all of this stuff, but I've never actually *done* any of it. I've never been anywhere. I've never even left the valley. I do all of the research and write the articles, but I don't have any real-world experience. I felt like I didn't have any credibility, so I created Josh."

James tried to explain about his youth, the death of his father, and life with his over-protective mother. Missy sat in stunned silence. He told her about Mr. Jessup and Simon, as well as the impact Rose's passing had on him. As he confessed the origin of the very clothes on his back, Donny approached with a tray containing a couple of bowls of stew and two cups of coffee.

"I think it might be time to sober the two of

you up," he said as he placed the dishes in front of them. "Things are looking a little tense over here. Sorry it ain't working out like I thought. Tonight was supposed to be a good time for everybody."

Missy looked up at him as he leaned in to place the coffee cups on the table.

"You knew about Josh?"

"Yeah," Donny admitted. "He told me the other day. Wasn't sure I believed him at first, but it made sense after I thought about it for a while."

"And all that building him up over at the bar earlier?" Missy had a blank expression on her face, a look Donny had never seen on her before.

"Yeah . . . well." Donny words dripped with guilt. "I was just trying to help him . . . you know . . ."

"*Get laid*?" Missy sounded a little pissed.

Donny blushed, his face turning almost as red as his beard.

"I . . . um, I gotta' go back to work."

With that, Donny retreated back across the room like a dog with his tail between his legs.

The conversation came to a halt as the pair started eating. Even in the noisy crowded bar, Missy could feel the silence between them.

Why do I even care? She thought. *It isn't like this guy owes me anything.*

And yet she did care . . . and it really

bothered her. It was James, who felt quite sober now, who finally broke the silence.

"I'm really sorry," he said sheepishly. "It's not Donny's fault. I just wanted to meet someone, anyone. He was just trying to help."

"Yeah, I know," she replied as she looked down, poking her spoon at the chunks of meat and potato in her bowl. "I can't really blame him. I mean it's not like I'm a virgin or anything. I guess I kind of have a reputation."

"That's really not why I came in here tonight," James said trying to sound reassuring. "And I don't care about your reputation. I just wanted to make a friend. Since my mother died, I've pretty much been lost without anyone to talk to. Donny and his mom are the only friends I have."

James pulled his phone out and showed her his contact list.

"I guess I came here because it's the only place where anybody seems to care what happens to me."

Missy looked up slowly.

"I care, don't ask me why, but I do. I don't even care about myself, but for some reason I think I actually care about what happens to you."

James shrugged. "That's okay, you don't have to say that. I know you're just being nice."

"Me?" Missy smirked. "Ask any guy in here. I'm never *just nice*."

She picked his phone up off the table, pressed a few buttons, and then handed it back to him.

"Any time you feel like nobody cares, you call me," she said.

James looked at his contact list. A fourth name now appeared. He smiled as he read it out loud.

"Missy Franklin."

Chapter 10

The winter sun streamed through the big living room window and painted the hardwood floor with light. James finished cleaning up after lunch and returned to his desk. For the first time in months the blinds had been lifted and the curtains pulled back, allowing natural light to flood the room. In the world surrounding James McCarthy, everything seemed a little brighter today.

His recently acquired phone spent the morning right next to his keyboard where he could watch it closely for any hint of communication from the outside world. Every once in a while, he opened the contact list and read the names, which had now grown by one — a woman's name — Missy Franklin. The very thought of it brought a smile to his face.

She wasn't just any woman, but a beautiful woman — the one female in that bar that every unattached male present probably dreamed about hooking up with. For some reason, she chose to spend the evening in his company. Much to Donny's dismay, however, they did not leave the bar together and spend a night of passion. Instead they sat in the corner booth and talked for hours.

During that time James did most of the

talking, answering the endless stream of questions coming from the other side of the table. Missy wanted to know everything there was to know about Jimmy McCarthy and the adventurous Josh McDaniel. As the evening went on, the questions became less about Josh and more about Jimmy, who by now had given up the new moniker and returned to being James.

One thing did bother him a little bit. Every time James asked Missy something about her past, she would deflect the question and bring the subject back to him. The dark-haired young lady with sapphire blue eyes seemed reluctant to share, and remained a mystery for the most part, but James vowed to keep trying.

Just when it appeared she would open up and give him a glimpse into her history, Donny sent up a flare. Margie left the hospital and was only minutes away from showing up at the pub. Seeing the two of them together would have sent her blood pressure through the roof and caused a huge scene. It wouldn't have ended well for all involved. The pair decided rather than deal with his new mother, it would be safer to call it a night and go their separate ways, picking up the conversation at a later date.

James was sitting at his desk, happily anticipating that conversation when the chiming of the doorbell broke the silence. The unexpected noise startled him so much he almost tipped his chair over when he jerked back to reality. The sound of the chime had become a rare occurrence in the McCarthy house. James no longer depended on home delivery for most of his needs. He now preferred the experience of shopping in actual stores surrounded by real people, rather than his past habit of relying on the virtual marketplace and packages being dropped on his doorstep.

As he approached the door, James got a look through the window at the man standing on his front step. His reddish-brown hair spilled out from under a dirty blue baseball cap, landing on his sloping shoulders. Even though he slouched, the stranger still appeared to be a little taller than James. Reluctantly, he unlocked the door and opened it. The face staring back at him looked faintly familiar, but he couldn't place it.

"You James McCarthy?" The stranger barked. "Or should I ask for *Josh McDaniel.*"

James swallowed hard. "I'm James. Josh is . . ."

The ragged looking man cut him off mid sentence.

"Yeah, I know Josh ain't real." He scowled, flipping his wallet open and waving a badge in James' face. "Detective Dugan, Detective *William*

Dugan! We need to talk."

James stumbled and almost fell as he quickly backed away from the door. The detective straightened his posture and stepped through the opening, presenting a much more imposing figure than before. His knees weak, James sunk into the wingback chair that blocked his retreat. His new lower vantage point made the man look even larger. He almost soiled himself when William Dugan closed the door with a loud slam.

"So, what's your angle?" He growled. "What exactly are you trying to get out of *my* family?"

The face finally clicked in James' brain. The detective bearing down on him looked like a slightly smaller, rougher version of Donny. This had to be Margie's youngest son, Will. No one had bothered to mention he was a police officer.

"Excuse me?" James tried to sit up in the chair as he responded to the accusation. "We're just friends. I don't want anything from Mom and Donny!"

Will barked back. "*She's not your mother!*"

"I . . . I'm sorry, but that's what she said to call her," James retorted. "And *I'm* not really comfortable with it either."

"Yeah?" Will's voice came down a notch as he responded. "Well, *don't* get comfortable with it.

Mom tries to adopt every stray that comes along, and I'm getting tired of running interference. I don't take too kindly too threats to my family."

James stood up and spread his arms. "Do I *look* like a threat?"

"Just what do you think a threat looks like?" Will asked as he plopped down on the couch. "I've been shot at by a 15-year-old kid and stabbed in the arm by a little old lady with a knitting needle." Will pulled up his left sleeve, revealing a scar on his forearm. "Everybody looks like a threat to me until I can prove otherwise."

"An old lady did that?" James looked shocked. "Why in the world would an old lady attack you with a knitting needle?"

Will grinned. "Because I busted her for selling oxycontin to the neighborhood kids, and she wasn't too thrilled about it. She was stealing it from the other people in her retirement home."

"Holy crap!" James was aghast.

"Yeah . . ." Will clearly enjoyed telling the story. "Holy crap is right. 83 years old and strong as an ox, but I had to applaud her creativity. I've never been attacked by a pointy stick with a sweater attached to it before."

"Unbelievable." James sat back down in the chair facing Will. "What can I do to convince you I'm not a threat to your family? I really like Donny.

I mean . . . well, he's really helping me come out of my shell. And your mother — she was there when I needed someone. I really owe her. I owe both of them."

"Yeah, Donny's a real teddy bear and Mom is a pushover. I'm not that easy. You want to convince me?" Will leaned back on the couch and raised his arms, lacing his fingers behind his head. "Tell me why I can't find a whole lot of information on you. I started digging for your skeletons as soon as Mom mentioned your name. She seemed a little too excited, and that got the hair on the back of my neck up. All I found is a couple of credit cards, a handful of online shopping memberships, and a Paypal account. It's almost like you don't exist."

"Well," James wasn't quite sure how to answer him, "I guess you can't find anything, because there's nothing to find. I've never really done anything or gone anywhere."

Will leaned forward again. "So, what's the deal with Josh McDaniel? Donny told me about your connection, but I didn't believe him until I checked it out. Hell, I found a shit-load more on him than I did on you."

"It's just my pen name," James explained. "A lot of writers use pen names when they first start out."

"Yeah?" Will growled again. "Well, in my business we call that an alias. It usually means you've got something to hide . . . and you're not just starting out. Everything I can find says you've been using that name since you were in high school. That's about 14 years now if my math is correct."

"Yes . . . I guess," James answered. "I created Josh because I figured nobody was going to believe anything written by a high school kid that never even left his own neighborhood. After a few years Josh had all of the credibility, not me, so I just stuck with it. I guess I didn't tell anyone because I figured they'd never believe me anyway."

"So why'd you tell Donny?" He questioned.

James frowned. "I was pretty hung over, and he's real easy to talk to."

"Okay." Will sat back again, sounding almost amused. "I'll buy that. If there's one thing my big brother is good at it's getting people to talk . . . and getting them hung over."

James nodded his head in agreement. "Yeah, your mom's pretty good at that, too."

Will laughed out loud. "Donny told me about that one. She hit you with hard stuff, didn't she?"

"I've never had coffee like that in my life."

James shook his head. "And I hope I *never* have it again."

"Yeah," Will agreed. "That stuff is nasty. You could drink paint thinner straight out of the can and feel better the next morning."

James' face left little doubt that he agreed. "I've never been so miserable in my life. Thank God for Miguel and his magic soup. That stuff is amazing."

"They fed you Miguel's menudo?" Will had an obvious look of surprise on his face. "Okay, now I *know* something's going on. What the hell did you do to get in so tight with them so fast?"

"I didn't *do* anything!" James insisted. "I got lost, I got cold, and your mom made me come into the bar. When she found out I had an Irish last name, she got all excited. When I said my mother had passed . . . well, I think she adopted me."

"Well, there you go." Will sank back into the couch. "The perfect storm—a lost, freezing Irish kid without a mother. You pushed every one of her buttons in one whack."

"I didn't do it on purpose," James protested. "And I'm not a kid. I'll be thirty-two in May."

"To her you're a kid," Will replied. "We're about the same age and she still calls me her *baby boy.* I guess it doesn't matter if you did it on purpose or not, it's done, but I still don't trust you."

James nodded. "I understand. You don't really know me, but if you give me a chance . . ."

"Oh, I'll give you a chance." Will leaned forward again. "But you're going to have to do something for me."

"Anything," James responded. "I really want to prove myself to you."

"You might regret that statement." Will pulled his phone out and sent a text. A few seconds later James' phone went off. "That's my number. Save it under the name *Willy D*."

James walked over to the desk and picked his up phone. He entered the name as instructed and saved the number.

"So, what do you want me to do?"

Will stood up and walked to the front door and opened it. He turned around and looked James straight in the eye.

"You just watch that phone. When I think of something, I'll let you know."

Chapter 11

The rest of James' weekend came and went without any further drama, but not without stress. Not only did he watch his phone for calls or messages from Missy, but also from his surprise Saturday afternoon visitor. He felt nervous anticipation as he waited for any communication from his new lady friend, but dread at the thought of Detective Dugan calling.

James tried to distract himself by getting up and doing odd jobs around the house. When that didn't work, he sat down in the living room and turned on the TV. The only thing that even halfway interested him was the news, but even that didn't last. The stories of murder and the rampant drug trade fed the fear his mother had instilled in him. He turned the TV off and vacuumed the living room . . . for the third time.

Finding no relief, James surrendered and sat down at his desk. He set his phone next to the keyboard and went to work but having the phone in his field of vision continued to be an issue.

As he eyed the phone, a question popped into his mind. Why did Will have him save his number under the name *Willy D*? Why not enter it as William Dugan, Detective Dugan, or just plain

Will? It didn't make any sense to James, but he wasn't about to question the man.

There must have been a good reason, He thought.

Seeing as how he hadn't earned Will's trust yet, James figured it safer not to ask.

Thinking about the detective again, James noted that Will Dugan appeared quite different from the rest of his family. Unlike his mother and Donny, who generally greeted the world with open arms, Will came off as brash, rude and suspicious of everyone. The man even sounded different. The other members of the Dugan clan spoke with a watered-down Irish accent. If Will had any accent at all, it was more of an urban vibe, like something you would hear on TV when news reporters interviewed a person from the streets of the inner city.

Will's appearance also stood in sharp contrast to his kin. His older brother, while not exactly a fashion statement, kept clean and well groomed, right down to his beard.

Will looked dirty, shaggy and quite frankly, he really didn't smell very pleasant. His funk continued to hang in the air long after the man left. Even with the cool January wind blowing outside, James felt the need to light some candles and open a few windows after his departure. The furnace was forced to work a little harder for a couple of hours while the air inside the little house cleared.

The only explanation that made any sense to him was that the detective must have been working under cover. If not, James reasoned, Margie would never have tolerated his lack of personal hygiene. She no doubt would have made the fact known in a physical fashion. The very thought of Will getting a head-slap from his mother, like one he had witnessed Donny receiving, made him smile. Holding on to that mental picture made the big, tough cop a little less intimidating.

James tried to ignore his phone and go back to work. Just as a watched pot never boils until you turn away, his phone announced the arrival of a text message within minutes of turning his attention back to the computer screen.

In a feeble attempt at humor James had set his alert signal to the sound of a sonar ping, as Margie constantly messaged him to check his location. He picked up the phone and was pleased to see a text from Missy this time, not from his new mother.

While he utilized email every day, texting was a new world for James. He found the tiny keyboard and broken conversations a little hard to get used to. James felt more comfortable writing a

116

complete, well crafted letter and receiving a carefully worded response at a later date. He found the short blurbs and syncopated nature of this new communication medium somewhat disconcerting.

MISSY: You ok? Haven't heard from you.

JAMES: Sorry, I was catching up on some things around the house.

MISSY: Caught up enough to meet tonight? Thought we might talk some more.

JAMES: Sure, but I don't think we should go to Dugan's. Margie might be there.

MISSY: Good call. We can go somewhere else. I know a few places.

JAMES: Ok. How does 6pm sound? I can pick you up.

MISSY: Perfect.

JAMES: I don't have your address.

MISSY: Gas station at the corner of 7th Street and Camelback. Pick me up there.

JAMES: Ok, see you at 6. Dinner is on me.

James was excited at the thought of seeing her again, but one thing did bother him. Why pick her up at a gas station? Why not at her house or apartment? He could understand if she didn't trust him yet, she barely knew him. If that was the case, then getting into a stranger's car wasn't exactly a smart move either. Missy seemed like a pretty tough character who, he assumed, could handle herself in most situations, so it had to be something else. Maybe she had something to hide, he thought, but what?

All sorts of possibilities began bouncing around in James' mind. Could she be homeless? No, she was clean, well dressed . . . and smelled heavenly. Maybe she lived with her parents or some relatives who didn't approve of her lifestyle? That seemed a reasonable explanation. Maybe she had a husband? That one terrified him. While James looked forward to experiencing new things, being chased down by a jealous husband and beaten, or worse, definitely did *not* make the list.

James did his best to get his imagination under control so he could focus on work. He decided whatever the reason, he would just have to muddle through and deal with the situation as it developed. That was the price of admission if he wanted to see Missy again. The woman had her secrets and didn't seem likely to give them up without some coaxing, so he had to be patient. He figured it would take time to gain her trust, but he was okay with that. In fact, he preferred it. The thought of things moving too fast felt a bit scary.

The rest of the day, however, did not move

fast enough. The afternoon felt like it would never end now that he had something to look forward to. Eventually the clock relented, freeing him to prepare for his evening.

Getting ready to go out was no longer a laborious process. Josh had very little input now when it came to wardrobe. James enjoyed his comfortable new dress code. Tonight he chose a pair of jeans, tucked the gray Henley in, and topped it off with the red and gray flannel shirt. A pair of black running shoes completed the look.

James grabbed his keys and headed out the door, locking it behind him. Somehow that door became less of a barrier every day. It now led to a whole new world of possibilities. It no longer kept life at bay but allowed him access to it. His world had expanded beyond the walls of his parent's house, as well as the confines of the neighborhood, and he loved it.

As James turned the car from his small street onto a busy major thoroughfare, he contemplated some of the other boundaries he was pushing. He wasn't just conquering physical boundaries, but mental ones as well. Many of the imaginary walls Rose helped to build around him were melting away. He no longer feared crowds or public places, and even the dark of night became less intimidating. As the walls fell, the sights and sounds of the city were no longer a part of some forbidden landscape, but a part of *his* world.

To him, every light in every window he passed now told a story. The writer in him tried to imagine the multitude of narratives he could pen if he only had a way to peer into the openings and eavesdrop on the conversations.

There could be stories of love, betrayal and mystery, as well as lying, cheating and deals gone wrong. He wished someday he could write *those* stories instead of just compiling statistics and reviews, and then signing Josh's name to them.

One story in particular interested him the most — the story of the woman who would be in his car in a few minutes. While he undeniably had a physical attraction to her, he was more curious to know about what went on inside Missy's head. He wanted to learn everything he could about the life that molded her into the person she had become, but Missy had walls too, and they were not falling as easily as his.

James grew nervous with anticipation when the station came into view. Standing under the lighted canopy he spied the figure of a woman, her shape silhouetted against the white body of a gas pump. She wore blue jeans and a red blouse, with a gray jacket topping it off. James shook his head . . . they were wearing the same colors.

His heart pounded in his ears as he turned into the driveway and pulled up next to her, hitting the unlock button, he brought the car to a stop. Missy opened the door and slid into the passenger seat, grinning as she looked him over and came to the same realization about their matching clothes.

James, who had been holding his breath, exhaled. He recalled that lonely drive home from the cemetery in September. The image of that empty seat had been seared into his brain, along with the lonely feeling that accompanied it. The wish he made that day had finally come true. Someone else was filling that space.

"Nice outfit . . . and you're driving a white, ten-year-old Buick four door?" Missy chided. "It's kind of an old lady car. I would have expected the great Josh McDaniel to drive an exotic sports car or something like that."

James grinned. "Yeah, I always imagined Josh in a Land Rover, right hand drive of course, but James is a little more practical. This was my mother's car, and it's almost *twelve* years old. It's a little like me, low miles and dependable, but it's never really been anywhere."

"You know I'm just teasing, right?" Missy flashed him a smile. "I mean, I don't even have a car right now, so I've got no room to bitch."

"How do you get around?" He asked. His curiosity was genuine.

"Most of the time I walk or take the bus," she replied. "I work close to here so I can walk from home, and the grocery store is only a few blocks away."

"Well, tonight this old lady car is your magic carpet." He was trying his best to sound like the suave and worldly Josh. "Where would you like it to take you for dinner?"

Missy eyed his flannel shirt, and then looked at her own clothes. "I don't think we're really dressed for Durant's. How do you feel about Mexican food?"

James nodded. "Works for me."

"Ok then." She pointed to the southwest. "How about Macayo's on Central? They make great margaritas."

"You know, it's kind of funny," James replied as he pulled back out on the street. "I've lived within a couple miles of that place all my life, but I've never been there. I wrote about it in a few restaurant guides and articles about the city, but I pulled all of my information off the internet."

Missy put a hand on his shoulder and smiled. "I guess this old lady car is your magic carpet, too. Maybe we should hit a few of the places you've written about so you can see if you were right."

James slid one hand off the wheel and placed it on Missy's.

"I'd like that," he said with a smile. "I feel kind of guilty sometimes when I turn in an article. For once it might be nice to be able to form my own opinion about some of this stuff based on firsthand experience."

"Well," she gave him a wink and squeezed his fingers, "If it's experience you want, I'm just the girl to give it to you."

James blushed and pulled his hand back, stiff arming the wheel.

"*Soooo*, you say they have good margaritas at Macayo's?"

"I'm sorry!" Missy laughed. "That came out *completely* wrong! I just meant I can show you around the city, you know, be your tour guide."

"That's ok, it's not your fault," he reassured her. "I just took it wrong. Sometimes I forget Josh is in my head and, well . . . he just goes to some bad places sometimes."

She smirked and shook her head. "Don't blame it on your imaginary friend. *All* guys think that way. It's just how you're wired."

"Yeah," James sighed. "I guess I can't blame Josh every time my mind wanders. I created him, so that stuff has to come from *somewhere* in my head."

"We all have that kind of voice in our head," she replied. "The only difference between you and everybody else is you gave *your* voice a name."

James grimaced as he looked over at her. "That's a little mental, isn't it?"

"Not really," she said smiling again. "We all had imaginary friends when we were kids, you just kept yours."

James nodded in agreement and turned the car onto the side street that led to the parking area behind the restaurant. After weaving up and down a few rows in the crowded lot, he finally located an empty space and threaded the vehicle into it.

"Looks a little crowded tonight," he commented as they opened the doors and stepped out. "I hope we don't have to wait too long for a table."

Missy was quick to reply. "We can hang out in the bar if we need to."

"Yeah," James rubbed the back of his neck. "I think I've had enough of bars for a while."

Heading toward the historic establishment, the couple walked side by side on the broken pavement of the aging lot. When they approached the back entrance, Missy stumbled trying to avoid a large crack in the driveway. Without thinking, James reached out and wrapped his arms around her, catching her before she ended up on the ground.

The two clutched each other as he returned her to her feet. With their bodies pressed tightly together, time seemed to come to a screeching halt. Their eyes met and James' stomach did a flip. His heart began to race, threatening to beat right out of his chest. He felt an overwhelming urge to do something. James wanted to kiss her. He slowly inched his face closer to hers and . . .

HONK!

The blast of a car horn jerked both of them back to reality. James looked around and quickly realized they were still standing the middle of the driveway, and the graying man driving the red pickup they were blocking didn't look too happy about it.

Chapter 12

Loud music flowed out from the cantina door as Missy and James passed by on their way to the main lobby. Happy hour was in full swing and the after-work crowd had the dimly lit room packed to near capacity. Instead of the traditional music he expected, James was surprised to hear a classic rock song thumping through the walls.

"Fleetwood Mac?" He said with a curious look on his face. "I would have expected to hear Mariachi or Norteño music. This *is* a Mexican restaurant, you know."

Missy shook her head. "Do they only play Irish music at Dugan's? It's the bar. They play party music in there. Don't worry, they play the other stuff in the dining room."

"You do know I was kidding, right? I guess I don't really have the whole humor thing down yet," he replied as they rounded the corner and approached the hostess station.

"Yeah," she said giving him a crooked smile. "We're going to have to work on that, but I'm impressed you recognized the band. Pretty good for a shut-in."

James laughed it off. "I'm socially stunted, not deaf."

Missy nodded. "Getting better with the jokes."

The dining area was nowhere near as crowded as the bar and the hostess was able to seat them right away. She led the couple to a heavy, dark wood table in the middle of the large, brightly decorated room. James pulled Missy's chair out as she approached it. She gave him a strange look and then sat down as he pushed it in.

"I didn't know guys still did that," she commented as he took the chair directly across from her.

James shrugged. "I didn't know they ever *stopped* doing it."

"Real gentlemen are becoming very rare," the hostess interjected as she handed them each a menu. "You're a lucky woman."

As the hostess walked away Missy muttered under her breath.

"I guess I am."

"What's that?" James asked. "I couldn't hear you over the music."

"Nothing," she replied. "Just talking to myself."

He cringed. "Please tell me you're not starting to do that too. One of us talking to the voices in their head is bad enough."

"Don't worry," she bantered. "I haven't

named my voices yet."

James laughed. "Yet…"

Missy eyed the menu. "Now I *really* need that margarita."

They both chuckled as a waiter approached the table and greeted them.

"Welcome to Macayo's. Would you like to start your evening with something to drink?"

"Oh, yeah," Missy replied enthusiastically. "I'll have a margarita on the rocks."

James looked quizzically at her. "Why on the rocks? I thought they were supposed to be blended, you know, like a slushy."

"Two reasons," she replied. "First, the ice melts slower if it's on the rocks so, it doesn't water down the booze as much."

"Ok," he nodded. "That makes sense. What's the second reason?"

Missy put a finger in the middle of her forehead. "Ever get a brain-freeze from one of those slushies?"

James and the waiter both laughed.

"I can't argue with that logic," he replied looking at the waiter. "I'll have mine the same way." He looked back at Missy. "We better order an appetizer too, or I'll be under the table before the main course gets here."

She grinned. "Ok, we'll have the green corn

tamale bites."

As the waiter walked away, James questioned his date. "What are those, little tamales? Do they come in a cornhusk like the regular ones do?"

"Ever have hushpuppies?"

"Yes," James replied. "Simon took me out to a dinner once. We went to a Cajun restaurant."

"Well," she said, "they're kind of like that, but sweeter."

"Ah," he nodded. "Deep-fried? I've heard everything is better deep fried."

Missy shook her head and made a face.

"Not everything. Have you ever been to the state fair? They have a place that deep fries everything. The deep-fried Twinkies are *disgusting*."

James looked horrified. "That even *sounds* awful."

"I'm talking from personal experience on this one." She stuck her tongue out and made a face. "I spent two hours in the beer garden trying to get the taste out of my mouth."

"I've never been to the fair." James looked a little down. "My mom always warned me to stay away from fairs and carnivals. She said you can't trust carnival people."

Missy leaned across the table and patted his

hand. "Man, your mother was a real stick in the mud, wasn't she? Did you *ever* have any fun?"

"I think fun left my mother's vocabulary after my dad passed." James was looking a little more serious as he spoke now. "Everything seemed to be about being safe and responsible, and just being good. When I was a kid, Mom had a lot of rules about good behavior. I didn't understand most of them, and I didn't want to do the wrong thing, so I usually avoided doing *anything*."

Missy sighed and lowered her head a little. "I guess she wouldn't have liked me any more than Margie does . . . maybe even less."

"I don't know." He shrugged his shoulders. "Maybe if she got to know you, but that's the problem. She never would have given you that chance. She never gave *anyone* that chance."

"What do you think she was so afraid of?" Missy asked.

Before James could answer, their waiter approached the table with the drinks and appetizer. They quickly placed their dinner orders and handed over the large colorful menus, eager to pick up the conversation where they left off. Missy raised her glass to her lips, licking a little bit of the salt off the rim before taking a sip.

"So," she said as she placed the glass back on the table. "Why do you think your mom was so afraid of everything?"

"I've actually been giving that a lot of thought the last couple of weeks," he replied pensively. "A whole new world is opening up for me now and I've been wondering why she never let me see it before. I think she might have been afraid I'd leave her . . . you know, like my dad did."

Missy reached for his hand again. "Your dad didn't leave her, he died."

"I know," James replied as he looked down at the soft hand touching his. "But I got the feeling she felt abandoned, like maybe it might have even been her fault somehow."

"How could it have been her fault?" Missy played with his fingers as she gently rubbed his hand. "You said he had a heart attack in his sleep, right? I mean, unless she poisoned him or held a pillow over his face, it was just his time."

"I don't know." Somehow Missy's touch made him feel safe talking to her. "It's like she thought God was punishing her for something, like she wasn't good enough. She really didn't seem to believe in God, but more of a karma thing. If you put bad out into the universe, you'll get bad back. I think maybe she felt like she did something wrong and that's why he was taken away. I guess she thought she was protecting me by giving me all of those rules. She wanted me to build up good karma, you know, so nothing bad would ever happen to me."

Missy smiled softly and looked deep into his eyes, like she was looking all the way into his soul.

"If that's the case, then you have a whole lot of good karma you can kill off before you have *anything* to worry about."

"I don't know about that," James said as he looked at the glass sitting on the table in front of him. "I seem to be going through it pretty fast lately. In the last couple of weeks, I've been drunk and hung over, lied, and replaced my mother with one who's a lot more fun . . . oh, and I left my dirty dishes in the sink today."

"Well," Missy replied with a smile, "those dishes might be the straw that broke the camel's back! I probably have just as much bad built up as you have good. I'll tell you what, you give me some of yours and I'll give you some of mine. Maybe we can balance each other out."

James raised his glass as if to give a toast. "I'll drink to that."

Missy raised hers as well. "Here's to a little more karma down the drain."

They both smiled and took a drink. As James swallowed his eyes grew wide. He looked down at the glass noting an area of the salted rim, now devoid of any crystals.

"Wow!" He exclaimed. "I *really* like that. The salt makes the flavor of the drink hit your taste buds like a hammer!"

Missy giggled as she leaned back in her chair. "You sure have an interesting way of saying things. I've never heard it described like that before. I think I need to hang out with more writers."

"You could do that," he replied looking deep into *her* eyes this time, "or you could just hang out more with *this* writer."

Missy blushed a little bit. "Are you sure you've never done this before?"

"Done what?" He asked as he popped a tamale bite in his mouth.

"You know." She turned her head to the side a little and gave him a look. "Are you sure you've never tried to seduce a woman, because you're doing a pretty good job right now."

James almost choked on the food in his mouth as he swallowed it.

"Really? I swear I've never even *tried* to talk to a woman before you came up to me the other night. If I hadn't been drinking, I'm not sure I could have done it then either."

"I find that really hard to believe." She spoke with a kind of dreamy look on her face. "I've read a bunch of the travel stuff you've written. The way you describe the clubs, the beaches, the restaurants . . . you make women want to pack a suitcase and follow you anywhere in the world."

"That's not me," James replied. "That's Josh."

Missy shook her head. "But you *are* Josh, aren't you? I mean, you wrote that stuff, you just put another name on it, right?"

"Yes." James wasn't quite sure what to say. "I write the words, but not as me. I try to imagine what it would be like if I was someone else, you know, someone cooler like Josh. I guess it's kind of like living out a fantasy."

"It's still *your* words," she argued. "That all comes from somewhere in your head. That wasn't Josh talking a minute ago."

James pointed down at his drink. "That was the alcohol talking."

Missy protested again. "You've only had a couple of sips and it hasn't even had a chance to hit you yet. Face it Jimmy, you're smoother than you think. You've got the tools, you just don't have any experience using them."

"I guess you're right," he replied a little reluctantly. "But you're kind of easy to talk to. If I had to walk into that bar right now and start a conversation with a stranger, I'd freeze up like

Alaska in the winter."

"See?" She said excitedly. "*That's* what I'm talking about. You could have said you wouldn't be able to talk, but instead you used your words to make me *feel* it, not just hear it."

James took another sip, licking the salt from his lips before he spoke. "Ok, but that still doesn't help me start a conversation. If you hadn't approached me, we probably wouldn't be talking right now. I'm not even sure I could have kept talking to you that night without Donny pushing me out there."

"It's a good thing Donny's already married," she laughed. "He isn't nearly as charming as he thinks he is. If he wasn't there, I still would have kept at you until you talked to me. In case you haven't noticed, I'm a little bit pushy and not exactly shy."

James smiled. "Yeah, I have to admit I did notice that, but truth be told, I really don't know very much about you. All we seem to talk about is me."

"Believe me, I'm not nearly as interesting," she retorted as she scanned the room. "Oh look, here comes dinner!"

James shook his head as the waiter passed by their table, delivering the plates to a couple in one of the booths.

"Nice try," James replied giving her a sly grin. "It's your turn now. You've heard the James McCarthy story, now I want to hear about Melissa Franklin."

"First of all," she corrected, "don't call me Melissa, call me Missy. My parents only called me Melissa when they were pissed about something, which was pretty much all of the time."

"Ok," he replied. "Missy it is. So, I take it you had some issues with your parents?"

She shifted uncomfortably in her seat. "I think it was more like they had some issues with me. I mean, they always seemed to be mad at me about something. Most of the time, I had no idea what they were yelling about, so I'd just go to my room until they calmed down. Sometimes when things got really bad, I'd sneak out and go to my friend Stacy's house. Her mom was pretty cool. She'd let me spend the night there."

James looked shocked. "Didn't your parents worry when you didn't come home?"

Missy shrugged her shoulders, then leaned back, and crossed her arms. "They never even knew when I left. It's not like they ever checked on me. I could have been gone for a week and I'll bet no one would have noticed."

"I'm sorry." James looked down and sighed. "I really thought I had it tough, but I guess it wasn't so bad."

"Don't sweat it." She sat back up and reached for her drink. "Everybody has stuff like that growing up. Mine wasn't any worse than yours, just different. It all sucks. Can we talk about something else now?"

"Yes," he replied quietly. "I really didn't mean to bring the party down. I guess I still have a long way to go when it comes to social skills."

She leaned in again and took his hand. "You didn't do anything wrong, I'm the one with the problem. You know, I've never said that stuff out loud before and it's kind of scaring me that I'm doing it now. This is all new to me, too."

"Okay." He squeezed her hand and looked her in the eyes. "Let's make a deal. Neither one of us has to talk about anything we don't want to. We'll just have a good time tonight and forget about the past. We can talk when we're both ready."

Missy smiled. "Deal."

As dinner arrived, the conversation turned to less controversial subjects like favorite foods and colors. While they ate, James attempted to impress her with his knowledge of the history behind the restaurant and its founders, as well as other trivia he had managed to unearth while researching the area for some of his travel reviews.

They both seemed to be fairing better with the lighter conversation, even letting some laughter creep back into the dialogue. Just as the meal wound down, the now familiar sonar ping of James' phone announced the arrival of a text message.

"Margie?" Missy inquired with a smile. "She probably knows we're together. I'm sure she felt a disturbance in the fabric of the space-time continuum."

James laughed as he pulled the phone out of his pocket and looked at the screen. His smile disappeared and the color drained from his face. He read the name out loud.

"Willy D . . ."

Chapter 13

The sudden change in James' mood caught Missy off guard. The look in his eyes was obvious. Anyone would have recognized it right away as fear.

"Are you ok?" She asked as she freed the phone from his shaking hand. "Who the hell is Willy D?"

James heard her speak, but her voice sounded like it came at him through a tunnel. He couldn't make his mouth form the words to answer. His brain had locked onto the message he just read.

WILLY D: Time to prove yourself. Parking garage. 1st street and Van Buren. 1 hour.

"*Jimmy!*" Missy slapped the back of his hand, breaking him out of his shock. "Who the hell is Willy D and what does he mean about proving yourself?"

"Detective Dugan," James replied with a tremble in his voice. "It's detective William Dugan."

"Will? Donny's little brother?" She scowled as she spoke. "What the hell does *that* jackass want? You don't have to prove anything to him!"

James shook his head. "Yes, I do. He doesn't trust me. He came to my house Saturday. He thinks I'm out to take advantage of his mom. He wants me to do something for him to prove I'm for real, not just conning Margie and Donny."

"*That bastard!*" She held his phone up and started to type. "I'm telling him he can go *fuck* himself!"

"NO!" James grabbed the phone out of her hand. "*Please* don't do that!"

"Why not?" She said, still scowling. "He's an asshole and a bully. He doesn't care about you. He just wants to use you."

"He's just trying to protect his family," James protested. "I need to prove that I'm not a threat and he can trust me."

"Yeah, right." She didn't bother to hide the disgust in her voice. "He's a cop. He had to know you weren't a threat as soon as he met you. A third grader could see that. He's just yanking you around so he can get what he wants out of you. That's how he works."

James shrugged his shoulders. "Maybe so, but I've still got to find out what he wants. I can't just blow him off. He could ruin things with the rest of his family, and I don't want that to happen."

"Fine!" Missy put her hands on the table

and pushed her chair back as she stood up. "Then I'm going with you."

James managed a little smile as he flagged down their waiter. "Don't you think I should pay the bill first?"

Missy plopped back down in the chair, teeth clenched and arms crossed like a child who had been told she couldn't leave the table until she ate her vegetables. She glared at James.

"Not funny . . ."

After he paid the check, the two of them headed out the back door toward the parking lot. Missy still appeared upset and remained quiet. When they reached the car, James broke the silence.

"You don't have to come with me, you know," he said as they both buckled in. "I have time to take you home before I head down there."

"Like hell you will," she responded with a growl in her voice. "I don't know what that son of bitch is putting you in the middle of, but I'm not about to let you go down there alone."

"Okay." James started the car and pulled out of the lot. "I've already learned not to argue with you. I'm guessing you really don't like him. Did he do something to you?"

"Let's just say we don't get along," she responded, with venom in her voice. "And leave it at that for now."

"Consider it left." James said, turning south on the main drag.

As he piloted the car down Central Avenue, his mind was going in multiple directions. One part of him felt nervous and fearful, wondering what he would be facing once he reached the dark parking garage. At the same time, another part was curious about the history between Will and Missy. He longed to know what had her so wound up. James wanted to press her for the details, but he figured he shouldn't push it based on their earlier conversation. All he could do was wait until she was ready to talk.

He turned the radio on low to fill the silence. Missy sat like a statue, arms still crossed and a frown carved deep into her face. As the car passed below each streetlight, the shadows cast by the changing angles of their illumination appeared to make her unflinching features move. He found himself unconsciously adjusting the speed of the car to make the rhythm of the lights match the beat of the music.

When the two stimuli finally synchronized, it looked like she was dancing with the shadows. In that little slice of time, James felt like he witnessed motion without movement, and poetry without words. He saw beauty in the darkness he once feared . . . and then the moment slipped away.

As James made the left turn off First Avenue and onto Van Buren, the reality of his situation came flooding back. The parking structure and what waited inside were only two short blocks away. The chill of the evening wasn't enough to stop the beads of sweat forming on his brow. He reached over and turned the radio off as he rounded the corner and approached the garage entrance.

"Well, we're here," he said in a low voice. "We're a little early and he didn't say where in the garage we were supposed to meet. I guess I should call him."

"You could do that," she responded, still stone-faced. She uncrossed her arms and pointed to her right. "Or you could just pull over there by that guy waving like an idiot."

James shook his head, swung the car around, and headed for the tall figure half hiding behind a concrete pillar. As he parked, his headlights settled on the man revealing his identity. Will Dugan still wore the same clothes he had on during his visit to the McCarthy household two days earlier.

Nervous, James fumbled for the switch to roll his window down as the detective stepped around toward his side of the car. The glass descended into the door. The same rancid cloud of body odor that assaulted his senses during their previous meeting hit him square in the face. Not only had the man done nothing about his personal hygiene since Saturday, but he somehow managed to make it worse.

"You should have come alone," Will growled.

Before James could speak Missy leaned over, extended her middle finger and growled right back.

"Bite me, Asshole!"

Will jumped back and lowered his head to look in the window.

"Oh, HELL no!" He yelled, pounding his fist on the roof of the car. He straightened back up. "What the fuck is *she* doing here?"

Missy fired back, pointing at James as she opened the car door and hopped out.

"Making sure you don't do anything to get him hurt!"

"Damn it!" Will turned back toward James. "Why did you have to bring that smartass barfly to be your guard dog?"

He opened his mouth to respond, but Missy beat him to the punch again.

"Smartass barfly? Really? Is that all you've got? I'd rather be a *smartass* than a *dumb ass*! And speaking of *ass* . . ." She pinched her nose and rounded the back of the car. "That's *exactly* what you smell like. Are you allergic to soap and water now?"

"I'm undercover," Will protested, He backed away from her, like a man retreating from a wild animal. "And I don't need you getting in the way. I'm trying to work a case here!"

James jumped out of the car and managed to head Missy off before she reached her target. As he held her back, he finally got a few words in.

"*Will you two stop it!*"

Both of the combatants froze in their tracks, the same look of shock on their faces. James spoke lower this time and very sternly.

"I don't know what the problem is between you two, and I don't really care right now. I just want to know what I'm doing in this garage and what it has to do with your case. And talk fast," James added. "I can't take this smell much longer."

Will and Missy looked at each other and then back at James. After a few seconds the detective cracked a smile and addressed the still serious looking man in front of him.

"Well if you don't like the smell, then help me close this damn case so I can burn these clothes and take a shower."

Missy interjected again. "And just how is he

supposed to do that?"

"If you'd *shut up* for five minutes, I'd tell him!" Will responded and then turned back to James. "Why the hell did you bring her?"

James shrugged his shoulders. "We were having dinner when you texted me. I was going to take her home before I came, but she insisted on coming with me."

"Yeah," Will nodded. "She's not very good at taking no for an answer."

"Hey!" Missy had that pissed off look again. "Do you remember the last time we met?"

Will dropped his hands down to cover his crotch as he twisted his knee sideways. James' eyes grew wide at the big man's reaction to the petite woman's words. Will's body language told a very clear story of his last encounter with Missy, and it looked have been be a painful one. James even noted what he thought might be a little bit of fear in the man's eyes.

"You keep a short leash on her," Will demanded pointing a finger at James. "I don't have time for this shit right now."

Missy looked geared up and ready to respond, but James beat her to it this time.

"Hold on, Missy," he said with his hand held up in stop gesture.

She closed her mouth and backed off,

leaning against the rear fender of the car.

"I have no idea what you think I can do for you," James said, turning back to Will. "So just spit it out."

Will straightened his stance and faced James.

"Ok, this isn't exactly what I had in mind when I came by the other day, but I have a buy set up and I can't do it. I need you to go in for me."

"A buy?" James melted back against the car. "Like a drug deal?"

"Yeah," Will responded. "One of my informants set it up, but I can't go to the meet."

James looked scared and puzzled at the same time. "Why not?"

"Because I might be recognized." Will kicked at the ground as he spoke. "I know a couple of the guys that do muscle work for this dealer because I've busted them before. If even one of those guys is there, the deal is screwed."

"You want *him* to do the buy?" Missy stood up straight and waved her hands in the air. "You can't send him into something like that cold. He doesn't know how to talk to those people. You're going to get him killed!"

"I don't have a lot of choice here!" He barked back.

James looked like a deer caught in the

headlights. *"Do I have a choice?"*

"You're the one that wanted to prove himself," Will quickly responded. "So, here's your chance. Believe me, you're about the *last* person I trust to not screw this up, but I'm running out of time and options here . . . and I already used your name"

"*YOU WHAT?*" James clenched his fists and took a step towards Will. "You used *my* name?"

Missy intervened this time, grabbing James by the back of his pants to stop his forward motion. Will shuffled backwards quickly to escape his advance. Even in the low light of the garage he could see James' face flush with anger.

"I was backed into a corner," Will admitted. "I had to come up with something fast. I needed a name that could pass a background check if somebody decided to look into it."

James gritted his teeth. "So, you pushed *me* under the bus?"

Will threw his hands up. "Hey, I needed a clean identity. I figured if I couldn't find anything on you, no one else could either. Hell, other than a shitty driver's license photo, I couldn't even find a picture of you."

"I can't believe this," James proclaimed, turning back toward the car. "You just figured I'd go along with this?"

"No." Will shook his head. "I wasn't planning on sending you in there, I was just going to use your name, but that went south when I found out who the dealer was."

"You *fucking* idiot!" Missy exclaimed. "Do you *ever* engage your brain before you put your mouth in gear?"

"You stay out of this!" Will shot her a dirty look, then turned back toward James. "Well?"

James stood silent, looking first at Missy and then at the detective, then back at her again. A knot formed in his stomach as he contemplated his options. One part of him wanted to jump back in that car and drive away, tires squealing while he put as much distance as he could between himself and that garage. Another part of him didn't want to disappoint his new family or the beautiful, spirited young woman staring back at him. As he looked deep into her eyes a familiar voice spoke in his mind.

It's ok Jimmy boy, we can do this!

A strange calm came over James. Hearing Josh's strong, reassuring voice brought him a sense of relief. If he took this job, he was going to need every bit of swagger Josh could provide. He straightened himself up and faced Will Dugan, tall and confident this time. James spoke only two words.

"I'm in."

Chapter 14

James planted himself on a concrete parking block, elbows on his knees and his head in his hands. Missy stood behind him, rubbing his shoulders as she glared at Will. The detective paced about twenty feet away, his back to the pair as he talked on the phone.

"You don't have to do this," she said quietly. "It's not too late to tell him to go find another patsy."

"No," James replied without lifting his head. "I can't back out. This is my family now and you do whatever you have to for family, right?"

"Yeah, right." She rubbed even harder. "If the rest of the family knew what he was doing, they'd kick his ass so hard his grandkids would feel it. My family wouldn't give shit if it was me."

James lifted his head and looked back over his shoulder at her. "I'm sure that's not true."

"You don't know my family," she replied, stepping over the block and sitting down next to James. "My dad couldn't care less what happens to me."

James put his arm around her shoulders and pulled her closer. "Every parent cares about their children, some of them just aren't very good at showing it. I always thought my mom was kind of smothering me, but I'm sure in her mind she was just protecting me. Sometimes I get a little angry when I think about all the wonders I never got to experience growing up, but then I think about all bad things that could have happened. I don't know, maybe I didn't really have it that bad."

"Yeah?" She laid her head on his chest. "Well, I have a feeling one of those bad things is about to happen."

"Maybe." Without thinking, he kissed the top of her head. "I guess if my mother could see me now, she wouldn't be very happy about it."

Missy looked up at him with a sadness he hadn't seen in her eyes before.

"I don't think either one of your moms would like this. *I* don't like this!"

"It'll be fine," he reassured her, even though he didn't believe it himself. "He's not going to send me in there without a plan or some kind of backup. I'm sure he has everything under control."

Missy shook her head. "If he had everything under control, we wouldn't be sitting here right now. We'd be sipping margaritas and dancing."

"Well," James grinned and hugged her tighter as he spoke. "Then I guess it's a good thing we got out of there when we did. I don't know how to dance."

Missy sat back up and smacked him on the leg just as Will turned around and pocketed his phone.

"You're lucky she hit you on the leg," Will said as he took a few steps closer. "She usually aims a little higher."

"Only when you deserve it," Missy responded, staring straight at Will. "I reserve that for *special* people."

"Well, it's nice to know you think I'm special," Will said with a grin, then turned his attention toward James. "Time to get serious now. Everything's set up, but we've got some work to do. You need to know a few things before I send you in."

James stood up and faced the detective, standing as tall as he could as he spoke.

"I'm going to need to know *a lot* of things before you send me in. Am I even dressed right? I'm all clean and shaved. I mean, look at you. You look like . . . you look like you just crawled out of a dumpster!"

"Smell like it, too," Missy interjected, turning her head away.

"You're fine," Will said looking James up and down. "You're playing the part of a courier.

You're just the guy that hands over a package and gets another one back. That can be anyone from some homeless guy just trying to earn his next meal to your seventy-five-year-old grandma supplementing her social security."

"Really?" James looked surprised. "I thought everyone involved in drug dealing was tougher than that. You know, all tattooed and nasty looking."

"You watch too many cop shows," Will said with a chuckle.

"I don't watch cop show," James replied. "Just the news."

"Anyone you see could be involved in the trade," Will pointed out. "Hell, you could walk in there in a three-piece suit and it wouldn't matter. Couriers are supposed to be invisible. They're not supposed to stand out. The best ones could pass you on the street and you'd never notice them. They just blend into the scenery. The guys that look all gangster and twitchy are the ones that get caught most of the time. The quiet ones fly under the radar."

"Yeah?" Missy stood up and planted herself next to James. "It may not matter how he looks, but it *damn* sure matters how he acts. If he goes in there all nervous and shaky he won't last two minutes. He doesn't have the attitude. Send me in instead. I know how to talk to people like that and . . ."

"*NO!*" James barked. "No! I'm not going to let you do that. Besides, they're expecting a man, not a woman. They're expecting to see James McCarthy."

"Not exactly," Will said looking around. "Nobody uses their real name in this business, but she's right about the attitude. You need to have some street cred. Everybody uses nicknames, so I just tweaked your name a little."

"You tweaked my name?" James looked confused. "You mean like that Willy D name you had me save in my phone?"

"Yup," Will replied. "I had you save it that way in case I have to call you in the middle of something. I don't want my real name popping up on your screen for the whole world to see."

"Ok, I get that," James said nodding. "So who am I now?"

"Let's face it." Will grinned through his scraggly beard. "*James* sounds like you're somebody's butler. I heard Mom call you Jimmy, but there's about a million of them on the street."

James shook his head. "You didn't use *Josh McDaniel* did you?"

"No way!" Will exclaimed. "There's too much information out there with that name attached to it, but I remembered your middle name from when I was checking you out."

"Raymond?" James replied. "You told them my name is Raymond?"

"Are you kidding?" Will laughed. "That's worse than James. No, I figured *Jimmy Ray* sounded about right. Kinda has a street ring to it."

"Kinda has a *redneck* ring to it," Missy sneered.

"Either way, it worked," Will replied. "They bought it."

"Great," The sarcasm in James' voice was obvious. "So now I'm a redneck drug courier named Jimmy Ray."

Will smiled. "With that flannel shirt and those shoes, I'd say you were more of a hipster if your jeans were tighter."

James grimaced and looked at Missy.

"I'm starting to think my mother was right about not hanging out in bars. Look where it's got me."

"Hey!" Will exclaimed as he extended his arms and spun 360 degree. "I was *raised* in a bar!"

James half smiled. "You're making my point for me."

"All right." Missy planted her hands on her hips. "Will you guys get serious? This isn't a joke, you know. If you don't get your shit together somebody's going to get hurt!"

"Damn," Will chided. "You look like my mother when do that."

Missy crossed her arms and leaned back against the car again. She did not look amused. In fact, if looks could kill, Will Dugan would have dropped in his tracks.

"Ok, let's get down to business," Will said turning back to James. "Here's the meat of it. There's a coffee house north of here where this is going down. All you have to do is drop one thing off and pick one up."

James looked at Will with doubt plastered all over his face.

"That sounds a little too easy."

"There's a few more details," he replied as he walked toward an old gray Ford sedan parked a few spaces away.

The detective opened the trunk, stuck his head in, and dug around for a few moments. When he emerged, he had a small black suede case in his left hand. The object looked like a well-worn Day-Timer portfolio. Closing the trunk and walking back toward James, Will extended his arm and handed the case to him.

"Go ahead," Will said with a little smile. "Open it."

James gripped the case by the spine and reached for the zipper that ran around the other three sides. As he slid it open a thick stack of well-worn one hundred-dollar bills began to emerge. His eyes grew wide and he quickly zipped it shut, pushing it back toward Will.

"Nope, you hold on to that," Will responded, shoving it back with both hands. "There's five grand in there. The bills are all marked and numbers recorded. If everything goes as planned, you'll be trading that case for another one just like it."

"I'm supposed to walk around this part of town holding *five thousand dollars* in cash?" James exclaimed. "Are you *trying* to get me killed?"

"Will you calm down, please?" Will shook his head. "Christ, if you keep announcing it like that you *will* get yourself killed. The trick to carrying a load of cash is to *not* look like you're carrying a load of cash. Just walk like you normally walk and talk like you just don't give a shit. If you act all paranoid everybody within a two-block radius is going to know you're hiding something."

"Don't act overconfident either," Missy chimed in. "That sends up all kinds of red flags. Put your mind somewhere else, you know, like you're just looking for a cup of coffee . . . nothing else."

James looked down at the case in his hand.

"How am I supposed to do that?"

"You do it all the time," Missy said as she took his free hand and looked up at him. "Every time you write one of those travel stories you do it. You imagine yourself in some other place and then write like you're living it. This is the same thing, but you're *acting* the part instead of writing it."

"Listen to her." Will looked at Missy as he spoke. "She may not be book smart, but she knows the streets."

"You're right," James said taking a deep breath. "I just need to act like this is a normal thing for me. I need to act like . . . like I'm Josh."

"Whatever puts you in the right headspace," Will responded. "Alright, here's what you're going to do. I want you walk in there like you know the place and order a cup of coffee."

James nodded. "Does it matter what kind of coffee I order? I don't really like any of that fancy stuff."

Will looked at the ground and palmed his face.

"It doesn't matter what kind of damn coffee you order! Would you just shut up and listen to me?"

"Ok," James responded sheepishly. "I just thought what I ordered might be some kind of code for drugs."

Will turned toward Missy, rubbing his

forehead.

"Is this guy for real?"

"You bet," she said with a smile. "One hundred percent noob!"

"Listen," Will said turning back to James. "Forget all the cop show crap you think you know and just pay attention. When you order your drink, the hipster dude behind the counter is going to ask you your name so he can write it on the cup. Tell him your name is *Jimmy Ray*, not James, not Jimmy, not Raymond . . . *Jimmy Ray*."

"Ok," James repeated back. "Jimmy Ray."

Will continued the briefing. "When you get your coffee, find a table and sit down. Put the cup on the table with the name facing away from you so anyone walking by can read it, and then lay the day-timer on the table in front of you."

"Really?" James asked with a little panic in his voice. "You want me to just lay all that cash on the table? Won't someone try to grab it?"

"You think somebody wants to steal your calendar?" Will replied sarcastically. "The only other person in that place who knows there's cash in that thing is the guy you're meeting. Now, *shut up and listen!*"

James nodded as Will resumed his instructions. "At some point, a guy will come up to you with the name *Marco* on his cup. He'll sit down and put another Day-Timer just like that one on the table. When he's ready, he'll pick up your case and you'll pick up his. *Don't* open the case—just get up and leave."

"That's it?" James questioned. "I mean, what do I say to this Marco guy? Are you going to be listening? Do I have to wear a wire?"

"No, you won't be wearing a wire," Will responded with a deadpan look. "Once you go through that door, you're on your own."

"*What?*" Missy did not sound happy as she took a step toward Will. "You're sending him in there without *anything?*"

"Relax, Missy," Will responded. "I'll be near by."

"No," Missy shot back, "*We'll* be near by! And why no wire? Don't you need to record the conversation for evidence?"

Will shook his head. "It wouldn't do any good in there. Between the noise level of the crowd and some Bob Dylan wannabe in the corner caterwauling, we wouldn't get anything usable anyway. I'm sure that's why Marco chose this place for the exchange. Besides, I already have him on tape making the deal over the phone. Once he has the cash in his hands, I've got the son of a bitch."

James looked even more nervous than

before. "What if *he* tries to rob me? Or something worse!"

"Don't sweat it," Will said calmly. "This guy isn't your normal street thug. He's smart, very smart. He knows if he pulls shit like that, word on the street travels fast. Best case, he's out of business. Worst case, they find him face down in a gutter tomorrow morning. He takes way too many precautions to chance screwing a deal that way."

"Precautions?" James felt the knot in his stomach get bigger. "You mean like a gun or something?"

"Oh, I'm sure he'll be armed," Will replied. "But that's not what I'm talking about. We don't even know who this guy really is. We've never been able to get a picture of him and he does shit I've never seen before. He's got one trick that's actually pretty genius. If he can't wear gloves without raising suspicion, he paints his fingers with glue. You know, that stuff you used in school? It fills the ridges and forms a kind of skin. It dries clear so you don't even see it unless you're looking right at it. I mean, we all played with that shit as kids, but this guy has taken it to the next level."

Will's eyes seemed far away as he talked about Marco.

"This bastard has managed to slip through

my hands more than once. This is just a small bust, but if I can nail him on it I know it's going to lead to something bigger. All I need is a clean set of fingerprints and I figure I can dig up his past. He may be a mystery now, but he had to start somewhere. Guys like him learn those tricks from experience, and experience means he's probably got a record. If I can get him into AFIS, his ass is *mine!*"

James could see anger rising in Will's face.

"Donny told me what happened to your father. I could be wrong, but this sounds personal,"

Will turned and pulled his collar to the side, revealing the scar from a what looked like bullet wound on his left shoulder.

"It *is* personal . . ."

Chapter 15

James sat motionless in the driver's seat of his car, staring at the coffee house half a block down the street. His hands were locked on to the wheel, squeezing it so tight no blood could work its way up to his fingertips. Missy reached over and gently touched his arm.

"Are you *sure* you want to do this?" She asked in a soft voice. "I wouldn't think any less of you if you backed out, you know."

"I would think less of me," James replied, releasing his grip on the wheel. "I'm finally starting to feel like maybe I matter. I can't blow that now."

Missy's voice grew shaky. "I just don't want to see you get hurt."

James slowly turned his head toward her. He could see the light refracting off of a small tear forming in the corner of her eye. He spoke softly, but more confidently as he reached out to wipe it away.

"Yeah, me neither."

A tapping on the driver side window interrupted their tender moment. James quickly snapped his head to the left and saw the now familiar, unwashed detective crouching beside the car. Will motioned for him to roll down the window. James nervously poked around in the dark for the button, finally locating it.

"I don't think he's there yet," Will said in a low voice. "But a couple of his goons are hanging around. I recognize one of them, so I can't step in and do this now. Are you sure you're ready?"

"Yeah," James nodded. "I'm about as ready as I'll ever be."

"All right," Will replied. "I need you to take your wallet and everything thing else out of your pockets and hand it over to your girlfriend. You don't want to be carrying anything that can identify you if you get searched. Just keep enough cash to pay for your coffee."

James complied, digging out what little he had in his pockets and passing it to Missy as he addressed the detective.

"Anything else?"

"Okay, just a couple more things you should know." Will's eyes darted around the area as he spoke. "There are four other officers in the area besides me. Two of them will be inside in case something goes sideways. Two will be waiting on the street to grab Marco when he comes out the door. I'll be covering the back."

"So, I won't be in there alone?" James breathed a sigh of relief. "That makes me feel a whole lot better."

"Well, don't get too comfy," Will responded, half smiling. "Those other cops have no idea you're with me."

"*What?*" James looked panic stricken. "So if this drug dealer doesn't shoot me, the *police* might?"

"*Keep your voice down!*" Will responded in a loud whisper. "This guy keeps slipping away, so I'm not taking any chances. I didn't tell anyone else who we're going after so word can't get back to him if he's got inside information. All I've told these guys is that a buy is going down and we're after *both* suspects, but mainly the seller."

James' face turned white as a sheet. "So you guys are going to arrest me, too?"

"Just *listen*, okay?" Will said with a slight growl. "After the deal goes down, you get up and head for the bathroom. Just slip out the back door and run south down the alley. I'll be the only one out back. I'm going to chase you for about forty yards. You drop the drugs and I'll stop to pick them up. That should give you time to disappear."

Will looked over at Missy.

"You take his car and park one street west of here. When he comes around the corner, you pick him up and get the hell out of Dodge. Got it?"

"I got it." Missy narrowed her eyes and

glared at Will. "You just make sure nothing happens to him, or you're going to have to deal with *me!*"

"He'll be fine. You just get his ass out of here when it's over," Will replied, turning his attention back to James. "All right, kiss your little bimbo goodbye and let's do this."

James turned toward Missy. "

This isn't exactly how I pictured our first kiss."

"Me neither," she replied softly. "I'll tell you what, let's save it until we're out of here and I'll *really* make it worth your while . . . deal?"

"Deal," James responded as he released his seatbelt and opened the door.

Will moved back, being careful to stay below the roofline of the car. James slid out of the seat and closed the door as quietly as he could. He had the worn black suede case clutched so tight in his left hand it looked as though his fingers were going to dig right through the leather.

"Ease your grip on that thing man," Will said, still crouching. "You don't want to look like your whole life is in there. Just hold it like you would any old book . . . and give your face muscles a break. You look like someone's already holding a gun on you."

James took a deep breath and let it out

slowly while Missy made her way into the driver's seat.

"You've got this," she said as she moved the seat forward and pulled the belt around her. "Just act like you're Josh."

James nodded his head. She was right, if there was ever a time for him to put on the persona of Josh McDaniel, this was it. He tried to push his own personality to the back of his mind, giving Josh the room he needed to take control. James straightened his back, loosened his grip, and made eye contact with the still crouching detective.

"Let's get this done," James said in a stronger, much more confident voice.

"Okay," Will responded. "Give me a twenty second head start so I can get into position and then head that way. Remember, you're *Jimmy Ray* . . . and try to keep it casual."

With that, Will slipped around the back of the car and disappeared into the darkness. As James stood silently counting, he felt a soft hand touch his. He looked down to see Missy's face peering back up at him.

"Be careful in there," she said firmly. "Trust your gut, James. If things don't feel right, get the hell out. We can deal with the fallout later."

"James isn't here right now," he said in a monotone. "My name is Jimmy Ray."

Missy giggled and slapped his hand. "Go get 'em, Jimmy Ray."

James stepped around the front of the car and on to the sidewalk, forcing himself to stroll at an easy pace as Missy drove off. He tried his kept his eyes locked on the coffee house. He did his best to resist the urge to survey the area in an attempt to spot the other officers Will mentioned.

James reached the corner of the building just as Missy's taillights rounded the corner at the end of the block and disappeared. As he approached the door, he mentally crossed his fingers, hoped for the best, and reached for the handle.

Stepping inside, the strong smell of coffee and spices immediately filled his nose. The tables were packed tightly into the space, nearly every one of them filled. A lone performer perched on a high stool in the back corner. He had a small PA system and strummed an acoustic guitar, butchering a Bob Dylan song, just as Will had predicted. James could hear Josh's voice in his head.

"Did somebody sit on cat?"

The service counter ran about halfway down the wall to the right of the door. Just past the end, James could see a small hallway leading to the restrooms and the rear exit. He noted the predetermined escape route and continued his survey. Two male baristas in dark clothing and tie-dyed aprons buzzed around behind the counter pressing buttons, pulling levers and generally making quite a commotion. They filled paper coffee cups and called out the names scrawled on the sides.

Working the register position, he saw a thin black-haired girl with more piercings than he had ever seen on one body. Her eyes and lips were painted black in contrast to her pale white makeup. Full sleeve tattoos covered her arms. A red dog tag engraved with the name 'Wanda' adorned her heavy, chain necklace.

When James approached the counter, she spoke in a very apathetic tone.

"Wadda ya want."

"Black coffee," he replied, trying to sound sure of himself.

"We have three sizes, sixteen kinds of coffee and 27 flavor add-ins," she whined, half heartedly pointing at the menu board on the wall.

James shook his head in disbelief.

"Just give me a sixteen-ounce medium roast. No add-ins."

"Name?" She said pulling the cap off a marker with her teeth.

James felt his stomach tighten as he replied.

"Jimmy Ray."

Wanda scribbled the name around the circumference of the cup and plopped it on the back counter. After taking his money and completing the transaction, she pointed to the other end of the counter just as unenthusiastically as she had the menu board.

"Pick up down there."

James threw his change in the tip jar by the register and walked to the end of the counter. Trying not to be too obvious, he checked out the rest of the room. Somewhere in front of him there two plain clothes officers, but he couldn't pick them out of the crowd. No one in the entire room looked anything like a cop to him, but then neither did Will Dugan.

That's the whole point of being undercover," Josh's voice echoed in the back of his mind. *Don't sweat the cops, Junior. It's the two apes Marco has planted in here I'd worry about.*

A cold chill ran down James' spine. Up until now, he had only been worrying about the dealer and the police. He'd all but forgotten the extra muscle lurking in the crowd. He scanned the tables once again, looking not for police this time, but people he suspected were closer to the other end of the legal spectrum. It didn't take him long to spot them.

"JIMMY RAY!" The barista called out loud

enough to be heard over the music.

Two faces sitting at a table by the front window turned to look. The men seemed over dressed, even for a cool winter night in this desert city. They both wore bulky jackets and dark stocking caps. The fact that they didn't remove either inside the heated building while drinking hot coffee, made them stand out from the other patrons.

Might as well have a neon sign over their heads with a flashing arrow! Josh observed.

Tucking the black case high under his arm, James turned back toward the counter to retrieve his order. With coffee in hand, he headed for an empty table against the back wall. He turned the back of the chair toward the wall and sat down.

The troubadour wailing away in the corner sat a few tables to James' right. The hallway and bathrooms were on his left. He figured this position gave him a good view of the room and more importantly, allowed for an unobstructed path to his escape route.

James took a sip of his coffee and placed it on the table, turning the cup until the name faced out just as he had been instructed. He laid the case with the money next to it. Not knowing how long his wait would be, James settled in and continued to scan the room. Less than two minutes passed before a short, stocky man in a well tailored suit approached the table and spoke.

"Crowded tonight, mind if I sit here?" He asked in a rough voice.

James looked up and saw the name *Marco* in large black letters on the man's cup. The case he gripped in his left hand looked very similar to the one already sitting on the table. Lifting his gaze higher, James was met by a pair of brown, bulging eyes so dark they almost looked black. Those eyes were set into a round face sporting a neatly trimmed moustache. It appeared to be the only hair above the man's neck apart from his eyebrows.

Just remember, the voice of Josh rang in James' head. *The less you say, the better.*

Agreeing silence was probably his best option, James simply nodded and motioned toward the empty chair with his hand while trying to keep a flat, emotionless expression on his face. Marco nodded in return, placing his case on the table next to the one Will had provided. As he pulled out the chair and sat down, James was able to get a good look at the man's hands. The tips of his fingers looked cloudy and slightly shiny. The glue covering his prints left no question in James' mind. This was the man he had come here to meet.

"Haven't seen you here before," Marco

said, trying to sound casual. "Is this your first time?"

"First time here," James responded, motioning toward the room.

Marco nodded and locked eyes with James, then lowered his voice.

"But not your first rodeo I'm assuming?"

James wasn't quite sure how to answer the question, but Josh did.

"Not really into rodeos," James responded calmly without changing his expression.

He couldn't believe those words had just come out of his mouth. He kept his eyes on Marco's, looking for any reaction to the sarcastic comment. Every muscle in his body tensed up as he waited to see if he needed to run for his life. Marco stared back just as intensely. Suddenly, the squatty little drug dealer broke into a smile.

"Not much of a talker. That's good business," he said shifting his gaze to the surrounding tables. "You never know who might be listening."

James nodded in agreement, still maintaining his stone-faced expression. The strong, silent thing seemed to be working for him, so he decided it best to stick with it—of course it also did an excellent good job of hiding the total panic he had going on inside. Marco took a sip of his coffee and then in what appeared to be a well practiced motion, placed it on the table again, picking up James' case as he retracted his hand.

"Thanks for the seat," Marco said as he stood up and pushed the chair in. "Enjoy the rest of your evening."

James gave him a nod with the same blank look on his face. He watched as Marco tucked the pack of money under his arm and shuffled toward the door. The two goons seated by the front window stood up and fell in behind him. When Marco reached the exit. James casually picked up the remaining case from the table and scooted out of his chair.

Aiming for the hallway, he noticed two more people were also on the move as well. One of the men headed for the front door as the other tried to make his way through the crowd toward James.

That's the other cops! The voice of Josh warned. *Time to exit stage left!*

James picked up his pace and he rounded the corner of the hallway, tossing his coffee cup in the trash can as he passed. The lighted 'EXIT' sign became his target—everything else in his view melted away. James hoped having to dodge tables, chairs, and people with hot beverages would slow the officer down enough to facilitate his escape. As he pushed the latch, the door swung open and the cool night air hit him in the face. He was out.

"Don't just stand there!" Will's voice rang out from the darkness. "*RUN YOU IDIOT!*"

Startled by the sound of the detective's voice, James could feel a surge of adrenaline shoot through his veins as the door slammed behind him. He turned south and ran down the alley as fast he could, tossing the black leather case toward a dumpster as he picked up speed. James heard Will's footsteps come to a stop where the package had landed. The plan appeared to be working.

Very little light illuminated the space behind the row of buildings, so James kept his eyes focused on the street at the end of the alley.

Just make it around that corner to the next block and this will all be over, Josh coached.

Once he jumped into his mother's old Buick, he and Missy would disappear into the sea of cars on Central Avenue. No more drug deals and hopefully no more Detective Dugan.

James made it about ten yards from the corner before a black sedan with a red and blue flashing light on the dash came to a screeching halt, blocking the end of the alley, and his escape. A large figure quickly bailed out of the driver's side door and pointed a gun over the roof of the car. James slid to a stop as the man yelled in a booming voice.

"On the ground . . . NOW!"

Chapter 16

The sidewalk in front of the coffeehouse exploded with activity as several police officers ran out of the shadows, guns drawn. A couple of them focused on the short, gruff looking man carrying a black case. The others headed off the two apish characters behind him as they tried to close in around their boss. All three men were on the ground in seconds.

"We got this handled," one of the officers yelled. "The buyer went out the back door. Somebody get around there and see if you can nail him down!"

"His ass is *mine!*"

Carl Stiverson jumped into a black Ford Crown Victoria and hit the lights as he slammed it into gear. He had two goals as he drifted the big sedan around the corner—catch the buyer before he disappeared and keep any of the officers *not* in the know from discovering his partner behind the building.

Carl brought the car to an abrupt stop, blocking the end of the alley. As he bailed out, he could make out a silhouette running in his direction. Carl pulled his weapon and pointed it at the figure.

"On the ground . . . NOW!" He yelled as he braced his arms on the top of the car.

Without hesitation, the man skidded to a stop and dropped to his knees. Will Dugan ran toward him, mumbling something under his breath.

"Get yer ass outta here!" Carl called to his partner. "I got this. You need to scoot before one of the boys in blue sees you!"

Will held up the case with the drugs. "You're going to need this. I found it by the dumpster, but he didn't have it on him."

"Just drop it and get moving," Carl responded, pushing the suspect down flat on the ground and planting a knee in his back. "I'll deal with it after I take care of this guy."

Will dropped the case and headed back down the alley, slipping in the back door of the coffee shop. Carl grabbed an arm and twisted it behind his prisoner's back, He slapped a cuff around the man's wrist and repeated the process with the other arm before grabbing the radio off his belt.

He keyed the unit and spoke in a deep, booming voice.

"Unit 3-1-2 David. Suspect is in custody."

***

Missy sat fidgeting behind the wheel of James' idling car. Her eyes were fixed on the sidewalk at the end of the block where a dim streetlight flickered while doing its best to illuminate the corner. Any moment now, she expected to see the figure of James McCarthy running in her direction. She checked the clock on the dashboard for what must have been the twentieth time . . . still no James.

When the ringing of James' phone ripped through the silence, Missy almost jumped out of her skin. That was about the last sound she expected to hear, as only a handful of people even knew James had a cell phone. She grabbed it off the passenger seat and looked at the screen. The name 'Willy D' burned on the display. She swiped the screen with her finger and answered the call.

"Why in the hell are you calling James?" She exclaimed. "Isn't he with you? He's not over here yet!"

"We have a problem," Will responded sounding a little out of breath.

Missy's stomach twisted. *"Oh God, you didn't get him shot, did you?"*

"NO!" Will yelled, trying to get her attention before her imagination traveled too far. "He's fine. It's just . . . well . . . he's been arrested."

"WHAT?" Missy almost dropped the phone. "How could you let that happen?"

"Everything went just like it was supposed to." Will took a breath and continued. "Until Carl came around the corner and blocked the alley. He had a gun on him and put him on the ground before I could do anything."

"So why didn't you tell Carl he's not a criminal?" Missy exclaimed. "Tell him to let him go!"

Will paced back and forth in the dark alley as he talked. "It's not that easy. I don't want to blow Jimmy's cover, *or* mine."

"Carl already knows you're a cop!" Her voice started to change from concern to anger. "And James doesn't need cover anymore . . . *right?*"

Will could hear the tone of her voice shift. "Just calm down, ok? Most of the plain clothes guys down here know who I am, but not the uniforms swarming around. As for Jimmy, he's got a clean record and I want to keep it that way."

"What if *James* tells them he's working with you?" She asked through gritted teeth. "He could blow your cover anyway. Damn it, if *you* don't tell them, *I will!*"

"If you do that, I'll make your life a living hell," Will shot back. "I got close enough to tell him to keep his mouth shut. If he doesn't say a word, they can't identify him. Right now, they've got nothing solid to hold him on."

"They still have him on the drug possession," she replied. "How are you going to get him out of that?"

"I've got that part covered," Will said with confidence. "He didn't have the drugs in his hands when he got busted. The cases are suede so they can't pull a print off those to connect him. He could have just been some guy walking down the alley at the wrong time."

"The two cops inside saw him make the exchange," Missy reminded him. "What are you going to do about that?"

Will had a response ready.

"They saw an average looking white guy from across a crowded room. I could put together a line-up they'd *never* be able to pick him out of. I also snuck back in and grabbed his coffee cup out of the trash so they can't pull prints and connect him that way."

Missy did *not* sound convinced.

"You've got it all figured out, smart guy. So they can't charge him, but are you just going to let him rot in jail until his 48 hour hold is up?"

"I don't even want to leave him in there long enough to get processed," Will barked. "We need to get him out before they print him and put him into the system."

"*We* need to get him out?" Missy went from angry to pissed off. "How the hell do you expect me to help get him out of a jail cell? I'm not a cop, and I'm sure as *hell* not getting arrested again!"

"Hey, that was an honest mistake. How many times do I have to apologize?" Will shifted the conversation quickly. "Do you cut men's hair?"

"*WHAT?*" Missy boiled over. "You get the only decent guy that's ever asked me out arrested and you want me to give you a fucking haircut?"

Will pulled the phone back from his ear as Missy continued her rant. When she paused to take a breath, he took the opportunity to get a few words in.

"Listen, Willy D can't just go waltzing into that police station, but Detective Dugan can. They won't even get him into processing until morning, so that gives me some time. I'm going to swing by my apartment, grab a shower, and chop this beard off. You get whatever you need to give me a high-and-tight and meet me at the pub."

"Fine." Missy's reply was curt. "But I'm not sure you should trust me with a pair of scissors right now. I might slip and *accidentally* cut your throat."

"Not a good idea," Will shot back. "I'm the

only chance you have of getting your new boy-toy back tonight." And with that, he ended the call.

Missy threw the phone at the seat where it bounced off James' wallet and onto the floor of the car. She pounded the steering wheel with her fists as tears started to well up in her eyes.

"*That son-of-a-bitch!*" she sobbed. "When this is all over I'm going to kill him and dump his body down a mineshaft!"

Slamming the car into gear, she wiped her eyes and pulled a U-turn, pointing the Buick in the general direction of home. She kept most of her equipment locked away in her station at the salon where she worked but, like most cosmetologists, she kept a full kit at the house to use on friends and off-the-books customers.

Missy made getting that kit and making it to Dugan's her only focus. Every time her mind strayed from her mission, she started to cry. The thought of James sitting in a holding cell with a bunch of gangbangers and drug dealers overwhelmed her. *She* knew how to deal with those kinds of people, but James? The tears started again.

***

James sat quietly in the back seat of the squad car, his hands cuffed tightly behind his back. He rubbed his face on his shoulders, first one side and then the other. Try as he might, he just couldn't get the last of the dirt out of his mouth. The detective who planted his face in the ground stood in the headlights of the vehicle talking with a uniformed officer.

Will's last words to him echoed in James' mind.

"Don't say a word to anybody. Don't even open your mouth. I'll fix this."

Yeah, right. Josh's voice rang through his brain. *He's the one that got you into this mess. Just get it over with and spill your guts to that big guy out there.*

"Not yet," James thought. "I can't blow Will's cover until I know there's no other way out."

Josh was persistent.

He probably set you up. He didn't want you around his family, right? Well unless they decide to stop by on visitor's day, he got his wish.

"I refuse to believe that." James continued the mental argument. "Besides, his mother would deck him if she found out . . . and she *would* find out."

I'm guessing that little girl you've been trying to impress might take it a step or two farther, Josh added.

James cracked a little smile as he recalled Will's involuntary reaction when Missy headed for him in the garage.

"I have *no* doubt."

The driver's door of the police car swung open and the uniformed officer made his way into the seat. As he set his notebook down, he glanced in the mirror.

"What are you smiling about?" The officer growled. "Cuffs not tight enough?"

James resisted the urge to speak as he straightened out his expression and buried his chin in his chest. Will said to keep quiet and, despite Josh's arguments, he planned to follow the detective's order. After a few seconds, the officer shook his head, fastened his seatbelt, and started the car. Jimmy Ray was headed to jail.

***

Will Dugan opened the door to his family's pub and stepped inside, presenting a much different picture than he had just an hour earlier. The bushy beard obscuring the lower half of his face was gone. He had his long hair, now squeaky clean, pulled back in a ponytail. Tattered and stained clothes no longer hung on his muscular frame. The detective now wore black jeans, military style boots and a white button down-shirt. His tan sport coat hung wide open revealing a brown leather shoulder holster containing a .45 caliber model 1911 handgun.

Ignoring Donny's waving hands Will headed straight across the room and through the kitchen door. He didn't break stride until he reached the back storage area. As he rounded the corner, he came to a sudden halt. Will found himself face-to-face with two *very* angry looking women. Donny burst through the kitchen door and skidded to a stop right behind him.

"I tried to warn you, bro!" Donny put a hand on Will's shoulder. "You really need to answer your phone when I call. Missy beat you here by fifteen minutes."

"An' she already filled me in," Margie said, stepping forward and kicking her younger son in the shins just above his boot. As Will bent over in pain, his mother applied a firm slap to the side of his head. "You're lucky your papa ain't here to see this. He'd tan your hide for sure!"

"Papa's a big part of why I do this job." Will straightened up, rubbing his head. "Can we talk about this later, Mom? I've got to get down there and clean this mess up."

"Darn right you're gonna clean this mess up!" She grabbed his shirt and dragged him toward a chair in the center of the room. "You sit yourself down right now and let this girl go to work."

Will slipped his coat off as his mother pushed him into the chair. Missy draped a cape over his shoulders and fastened it around his neck

. . . a little too tight for comfort. She stepped around in front of him and held up a shiny pair of barber scissors, turning them slowly so the light glinted off the chrome blades. Missy shot him an evil smile.

"You're *mine* now, Jackass. You better pray I don't miss and cut your jugular!"

Will swallowed hard as she moved behind him and grabbed his ponytail, snipping it off in one swift motion. She dangled it mockingly in front of his face before dropping it in the trash can. Margie stood directly in front of him, arms crossed and watched Missy work. Will had seen that stance many times. He knew the words of a lecture were lining up on the end of her tongue.

"You've done some bonehead things in your time boy, but this one takes the cake." Margie raised her voice over the buzz of the clippers. "What makes you think I need protectin'? Just who do think it was kept you safe when you were crawlin' around, soilin' your diapers?"

Margie uncrossed her arms and planted them on her hips. "And your big brother? You don't think he can handle himself? With your smart mouth, if it wasn't for Donny takin' up for you, you would'a come home from school with your nose bloodied at least once a week!"

Will opened his mouth to speak but she cut

him off.

"And now that poor motherless boy is sittin' in a cold jail cell havin' to fight off God knows who instead of havin' a nice evenin' with this young lady."

"I thought you hated Missy," he interjected.

Margie stomped her foot and waved a finger in his face. "Don't you be tryin' to change the subject, young man! I'm bettin' I don't have the whole story on that one either. You surely did somethin' to deserve what she gave you."

"He didn't tell you what happened?" Missy asked grinning like a Cheshire cat.

"All he told me was you gave him a swift kick in the jimmies," Margie replied, still staring at Will. "The boy couldn't walk straight for two days."

"He had me rounded up with a bunch of hookers last year." Missy dug a comb into Will's scalp, causing him to wince. "I had to spend the night in a cell full of un-bathed, over perfumed prostitutes before somebody finally told them to turn me loose."

Margie gave her youngest son a look only a mother could muster.

"You told me she was mad 'cause you wouldn't go home with her."

"You fed that shit to your mother?" Missy

dropped the comb and slapped the side of Will's head so hard he almost fell out of the chair. "You were pissed because *I* wouldn't go home with *you*."

"Can we do this later?" Will exclaimed, holding his arms up in a defensive position. "I need to get back downtown before Jimmy gets processed."

"Fine!" Missy whipped the cape off the still cowering detective. "I'm done with your sorry ass anyway."

Will stood up and brushed himself off. Grabbing his sport coat, he turned to address his mother. "You still keep the lost-and-found box in your office?"

"Yup," she replied through gritted teeth. "You lose somethin' besides your mind?"

He didn't bother to dignify her question with an answer. Will headed into the office and started digging through the box of castoffs and forgotten items. A few seconds later he emerged holding a gray hooded sweatshirt with the letters ASU emblazed across the chest.

"This should work," he said as he came out of the office.

He leaned over to kiss his mother goodbye. Margie grabbed his lapel in her tight little fist and pulled him down until the two were nose-to-nose.

Pointing at Missy with her free hand she spoke in a tone that left no doubt as to her position on the current situation.

"If even hair on that sweet boy's head is harmed, I'll hold you down while she takes care of business. You got that?"

Margie released her grip and Will stood back up. He straightened his jacket and tucked the gray hoody under his arm as he headed for the door.

"I'll let you know what happens, Mom." He called back over his shoulder. "Missy, hold on to Jimmy's phone and get back downtown. Be ready to move when I text you."

Chapter 17

The door to the squad room flew open and hit the wall with a thud. A tall figure sporting a military haircut immediately filled the empty frame. Without acknowledging anyone, he walked swiftly between the rows of low walled cubicles with his shoulders back and head held high. The lanyard holding his ID card and badge swung from side to side with every long stride. Detective William Dugan moved like a man on a mission.

Reaching the other side of the room, Will swiped his card through the reader next to the door and punched in his code. As the latch released, he pushed the door open and burst into the locker room. He made a hard left and then turned down the first row, coming to a stop about halfway down the aisle.

Dropping the rolled-up sweatshirt clutched in his left hand on the bench, he produced a key from his pocket and inserted it in the lock dangling from one of the lockers. Will popped the locker open and pulled the door back to reveal a space that resembled a teenage boy's closet after being told to clean up his bedroom. The locker was stuffed so full it would have taken an act of God to wedge one more thing in.

Will dug through the pile of shoes and boots tossed in the bottom, finally emerging with a small black tactical backpack. Tossing it on the bench, he dove into the upper section of the locker. This time his efforts produced a white t-shirt, a pair of dark blue sweatpants, and a lanyard with another ID card attached. The picture on the card was not Detective Dugan. He closed the locker, stuffed everything in the backpack, and headed back to the squad room.

Turning down one of the rows, he came to a workspace that looked much the same as the locker. He sat down and pushed a pile of paperwork to the side, making room for the keyboard perched on top of a pile of notebooks. He pulled the keyboard down and started typing with a speed quite impressive for someone using the hunt-and-peck method.

After a few minutes he logged out, tossed the keyboard back on the pile and spun around in the chair. Will grabbed the backpack once more as he bolted from the desk and headed for the door to the stairwell. He swiped his badge, keyed in his code, opened the door, and swiftly descended two flights, emerging in the basement.

Reaching into the pack, Will produced a baseball cap. He donned it, pulling it low over his face. He headed down the hallway and around a corner, disappearing into a service closet. Moments later he emerged and continued to the holding area, stopping at a door with a sign that read "Interview 7". The detective opened the door and stepped inside.

Will stood with his back against the front wall of the room, being careful to stay out of the camera's watchful eye. James was sitting at the lone table, arms crossed on its hard surface and his face buried. As he raised his head to see who had entered the room, Will motioned to him to keep his head down.

"Don't look up," he said in low voice. "I took care of the audio, but the video is still running."

James didn't say a word as he buried his head back into the crook of one elbow.

"You can talk now," Will whispered. "Just don't look at the camera. If somebody's watching they might see your mouth move."

James finally broke his silence for the first time in almost three hours.

"Who are you?"

Will crouched down so James could see his face without looking up.

"It's me, Will Dugan."

James lifted his head just enough to focus both eyes on the man in front of him. The voice sounded right, but nothing about him looked familiar. If it weren't for his resemblance to Donny, James never would have believed it was Will.

"What went wrong?" James asked in a muffled voice. "You were supposed to be the only one in the alley."

"Shit happens sometimes," Will replied. "I'm going to try to get you out of here. By the way, good job avoiding the cameras. I checked the security footage and it looks like they never got a shot of your face."

"I kept my head down as much as I could," he confirmed. "But I wasn't thinking about the cameras. I was just ashamed I was being arrested."

Will stood back up and checked his phone.

"Have you talked to anyone?"

"No," James replied. "I did just what you said."

"Good deal." Will let out a sigh. "I see you're not cuffed, so that eliminates one hurdle. Now I need you to listen closely and do exactly what I say. When I leave here, I'm going to tell the guard you need to take a dump. In a few minutes, somebody's gonna come in and take you down the hall to the head. I'll lock the other doors so he has to put you in the last stall. I'm gonna come out of the center one and distract him. You slide under the walls and come up in the first stall. Be as quiet as you can."

"You want me to crawl on the floor of a public restroom?" James was horrified.

"Would you prefer to be thrown in a holding cell with some bubba who wants to make you his bitch?" Will asked with a sarcastic tone.

James wilted. "Well, when you put it that way. . . "

Will held the black backpack where James could see it. "This pack will be on the back of the toilet in the first stall. You change into these clothes and stuff yours in the pack. Don't leave *anything* behind. There's also an ID card in the outside pocket. Put it around your neck and remember the numbers one-two-zero-seven, you got that?"

"Got it." James repeated the numbers. "One-two-zero-seven."

"Good," Will nodded. "When you're ready to go, put the hood on the sweatshirt up, grab the pack, flush the toilet and *calmly* walk out of the bathroom."

"Just like that? Just walk out?" James sounded surprised and concerned at the same time. "Where do I go?"

"Go to your left when you leave the room," Will continued. "The stairs are two doors down at the end of the hall. Swipe the card and key in the code to open the door. Go up one flight. There's an outside exit door on that landing. The smokers use it to sneak out all the time and grab a puff, so the alarm is disabled. They disconnected the camera too, so you should be in the clear."

"I'm breaking out of jail?" James sounded even more worried than before. "Where do I go once I'm outside? Missy has my wallet. I don't have any way to pay for a cab or anything."

"You're not officially under arrest, just being held for questioning, so technically you're not breaking out of jail," Will said with a crooked smile. "And you never take a cab when you're trying to escape. That's only about the fastest way to get caught."

"So, what am I supposed to do?" James asked sounding a little frustrated now. "Walk home?"

"I've got that covered," Will reassured. "When you come out the door, you'll be on the east side of the building. Walk, *don't run*, walk two blocks north and stay out of the light as much as you can. I texted Missy. She should be there with your car."

James gave a sigh of relief hearing a familiar face would be waiting for him, but he still had some concerns.

"What happens when they figure out I'm gone? I'll be a wanted man, won't I?"

"Just go home and lay low for a day or two," Will said confidently. "I'll take care of the details on this end."

With that, Will slipped out the door leaving James alone once more. He kept repeating the security code over and over in his head. The last thing he wanted to do was forget that number in the heat of the moment and end up trapped.

The door opened once more and James kept his head low, hiding his face. Peeking out from under his mussed-up hair, he could see the lower half of a uniformed figure. The man looked like one of the private security guards, not a police officer. James felt better knowing he wouldn't have to deal with trying to slip past a well trained, armed cop.

"On your feet," the guard barked. "Some detective said you had to take a leak."

James stood up, keeping his arms crossed and his eyes pointed at the floor. The guard grabbed him by the upper arm, marching him out of the room and down the hall. Holding the Men's room door open with one hand, he pushed James ahead of him and pointed him towards a urinal.

James had to think fast.

"I need to use a stall. I have to . . ."

"I don't need the details," the guard exclaimed as he cut him off.

Finding the first stall locked, the guard knocked on the second one.

"Occupied!" A voice shouted from behind the door.

Having success with the third stall, the guard shoved James inside.

"Just hurry up and do what you gotta do," he said in a frustrated tone.

James locked the door and crouched down, waiting for his cue to move. About twenty seconds later he heard the toilet flush in the next stall. The door opened and then closed again. The time to move had come, but the thought of belly crawling on that nasty floor was almost more than he could bear.

Just take off your flannel shirt and scoot on it, Josh suggested. *You're going to have to wash it anyway after being ground into the dirt in that alley.*

"Or throw it away and get another one," he thought as he pulled his arms out of the shirt.

"How's it going tonight?" James could hear Will's voice echo around the room.

The water running in one of the sinks covered the sound as the guard answered. James spread the shirt on the floor and quickly slid into the next stall. As he continued to move under the following wall, he saw the guard's feet pointing away from the exit door. From the position of Will's shoes, James could tell he had leaned against the back wall and was engaging the man in conversation.

Popping up in the last stall, James retrieved the pack from the back of the toilet. Rather than take the time to remove his shoes and jeans, he quickly stretched the sweatpants over them. Next, he slipped his shirt off as quietly as possible and replaced it with the white t-shirt, being careful not to raise his arms above the top of the stall. After donning the sweatshirt, he stuffed his remaining clothes in the pack.

James dug through the outside pocket of the backpack until he found the ID card Will told him about. He looked at his key to freedom and repeated the numbers again in his head as he placed the lanyard around his neck. James flipped the hood over his head and took a deep breath. This was it.

Taking the backpack in one hand, he reached out with the other and flushed the toilet. He casually opened the stall door and walked out of the bathroom without looking back at the two men still engaged in conversation. His heart pounded in his ears so loud he couldn't make out a word they were saying.

Turning left as instructed, James walked with purpose until he reached the door to the stairs. He swiped his card through the reader and punched in the numbers. Nothing happened. Nervous energy took over and the keypad became a blur. Try as he might, James couldn't recall the four digits standing between him and the outside world.

Josh invaded his brain again.

Come on, you remember that number! It's Pearl Harbor Day, for Christ's sake! December 7th!

"A date which will live in infamy," James remembered. "President Roosevelt said that in his speech to Congress the day after the bombing!"

Thanks for the history lesson, Josh echoed snidely. *Now could you please punch in that code and open the damn door before we get caught?*

He swiped the card again and keyed in 1-2-0-7. This time the latch popped. James wasted no time pulling it open and stepping into the safety of the stairwell, where he paused for a moment to breathe. One more door and he would be out, he thought as he slipped his arms through the straps of the backpack and pulled it into position.

He trotted up the stairs and stopped at the exit door. If Will was right about the alarm being disabled he would be home free, if not . . .

If not, you're screwed! Josh joked.

James pushed on the handle, swung the door open and stepped through. No alarm sounded. He turned north and immediately came face to face with two uniformed officers, almost colliding with them. Both had cigarettes hanging out of their mouths and surprised looks on their faces. James felt a surge of adrenaline like the one he had in the alley behind the coffee house. His fight-or-flight response begged to take over and send him into a full sprint, but something stopped him.

He raised his head and spoke in a very authoritative voice.

"Wipe those looks off your faces . . . *NOW!*"

The men straightened up and grabbed the cigarettes out of their mouths. James stepped past them, but couldn't resist giving them a parting shot.

"I'd better not find any butts out here in the morning or I'll have *both* of you on your hands and knees scrubbing the sidewalk!"

Josh laughed hysterically in his head as James confidently marched off into the shadow between streetlights.

That took some big brass ones! I think you may have picked up a few tricks from me, kid!

After making it down the block and into the shadows, James let out a huge breath and pulled the hood back exposing his head. He wanted nothing more than to feel the cold, night air on his face. The last few hours had felt like days and he knew the next few minutes were going to feel like hours as he covered the distance to his waiting getaway car.

James pressed on. Looking ahead, the familiar shape of his mother's old Buick grew larger causing him to pick up his pace. He could also make out the figure of a woman standing on the curb looking his direction. As he moved out of the shadows, he saw her jump and then run straight at him. James held out his arms and caught Missy as she leapt off the ground and wrapped her arms around his neck.

Clamping her legs tightly around his waist, she planted a huge kiss on the side of James's face before zeroing in on his mouth. The two stayed locked together for close to a minute before coming up for air.

"You have *no* idea how happy I am to see you!" Missy blurted out.

"I think I'm getting the picture," James replied with a huge smile on his face. "But don't you think we should get out of here before they figure out I'm missing?"

Missy released her grip on him and landed back on her feet. They both ran toward the car. she tossed the keys in his direction and headed for the passenger side. James caught them with one hand as he opened the rear door and tossed the backpack on seat. Jumping behind the wheel and starting the car, he looked at Missy and grinned.

"Your place or mine?"

Missy slid over next to James and took his hand.

"Yours . . ."

Chapter 18

The bedroom took on a warm glow as the midmorning light worked its way through the small spaces around the blinds. James rubbed the sleep from his eyes. The events of the previous night ran through his mind like a bad movie.

Maybe I just dreamed it, he thought.

Rolling away from the window to escape the light, he received confirmation that his memories were in fact real. He found himself spooning with the still slumbering young woman sharing his bed.

Missy stirred and snuggled up against him, squeezing a pillow in her arms. When she pressed her warm body against his, James came to a shocking realization—neither of them had a stitch of clothing on. Rolling away quickly, he pulled the covers up to his chin. After a few seconds, he slowly lifted the sheet and peeked under it, confirming his initial assessment.

As he sealed the covers down tight around his body, Missy rolled over facing him.

"What time is it?" She mumbled into the pillow.

"I-I don't know," James stammered. "I'm guessing it's got to be at least eleven, maybe later."

"That sucks," she yawned. "I really don't want to get up yet."

James wasn't quite sure what to say next, so he just went for it.

"Um, you know we're both naked . . . right?"

"Yeah," she responded casually. "Is that a problem?"

James bit his lip and looked at her. "Did we . . . you know . . ."

Missy smiled and put a hand on his arm. "You don't remember?"

"Well . . . um . . . it's just . . ." James was dumbfounded.

Missy winked and then let him off the hook.

"No, we didn't do anything."

James breathed a sigh of relief.

"I thought I'd lost my mind. I *really* don't remember a lot after we got home."

Missy let out a giggle as she woke up a little more.

"We were both totally shot by the time we made it back here last night. I dozed off on the couch while you were cleaning yourself up. When I woke up you were already in bed, so I just crawled in with you and went back to sleep."

James rubbed his eyes again.

"I'm sorry. I was so wiped out I must have

forgotten you were here. I think I just took off my clothes and crashed after I washed my face, but that doesn't explain why *you're* not wearing anything."

"You didn't think I going to sleep in my jeans, did you?" She said laughing. "I always sleep naked. I guess I was on autopilot too last night."

"So, what do we do now?" He asked staring longingly at his robe sitting out of reach on the chair by the bedroom door.

Missy sat up in bed and yawned. She stretched and the sheet and comforter fell away, exposing her all the way down to her waist. James froze with his eyes locked firmly on her breasts. Try as he might, he couldn't force himself to look away.

"We're all adults here," she said with a grin. She slid out of bed and stood up, facing a totally shocked James. "I don't know what you're going to do, but I'm taking a shower."

Missy turned and pranced around the end of the bed, grabbing the robe as she left the bedroom. A moment later, James heard the water running in the bathroom. He sat up on the side of the bed, still covering his now awakening 'private area' as his mother used to call to it.

Missy shouted from the bathroom. "Okay to use these towels, or are they just for show?"

Go for it! Josh encouraged, as James scrambled to get another robe out of the closet. *She wants you to come in there. The towel is just an excuse.*

"I'll bring you a clean one." He called back, trying to hide the nervousness in his voice.

"Bring two," she replied.

Josh prodded him again.

Now that's an open invitation if I've ever heard one.

James pulled on his robe and tied the belt around his waist before heading across the hall to the linen closet. He retrieved two large, soft bath towels and turned toward the open bathroom door. He paused as his eyes settled on the blurred figure behind the shower curtain. Now he had another problem to deal with. He looked down to see his fully erect penis pushing its way out of the gapping robe.

Missy peeked around the edge of the curtain and James quickly lowered the towels in an attempt to hide his ever-growing problem.

"Are you just going to stand there with your mouth open," she said licking her lips, "or are you getting in here?"

He hesitated for a few seconds and tried desperately to form words. "I . . . um . . . what I, um . . ." He finally spit it out. "W-what about, you know, protection?"

Missy giggled and pulled the curtain open

just enough for him to get a peek at her wet body. James fumbled the towels, sending them to floor, exposing himself in the process. He stood motionless, his jaw hanging even lower than before.

"You really *are* new at this," she said as she curled her index finger in a come-hither motion. "There are *a lot* of things we can do without protection."

James took a deep breath and untied his robe, letting it slip to the floor in a pile with the towels. Even Josh remained speechless as his creator slid the curtain back and stepped into the tub, pulling it closed behind him.

"I guess you're going to have to teach me," he whispered in a shaky voice. "This is one thing I *never* researched."

***

James was already dressed and had started lunch before Missy emerged from the hallway. She had her damp hair pulled back in a ponytail and the same clothes on that she wore the night before.

"You really need to get a blow-dryer," she joked. "But thanks for the toothbrush. At least my mouth doesn't taste like Mexican food anymore."

James placed two plates on the table and headed into the living room. He had an enormous smile plastered on his face as he walked toward her.

"I still don't know why my mom insisted on having so many extras around," he said putting his arms around her. "It's not like we ever had overnight guests. Actually, I don't remember ever having *any* guests."

Missy wrapped her arms around his neck and gave him a kiss. "Maybe she just figured someday her son would get lucky."

"Mom didn't believe in luck," he said as he returned the kiss. "But she did believe in karma, good and bad."

Missy reached up and touched the side of his face. "Well, I'm guessing you must have a ton of the good stuff. You've been a *very* good boy!"

"Yeah, but I'm burning through that pretty fast right now," he said with a laugh. "I've been drunk, I was involved in a drug deal, went to jail, escaped from jail, and this morning . . . well . . . I'm pretty sure we broke a few laws in there."

Missy dropped her hands lower and squeezed his butt.

"A few laws of nature maybe."

"That too," he replied with a huge smile. "I'm sure I've killed off a whole lot of good karma."

"You helped the police bust a drug dealer last night," Missy said as she danced around the living room collecting the rest of her belongings. "I think that moved the needle back a little."

"Let's hope so." James pointed at the table. "I made lunch. How do you feel about grilled cheese sandwiches and tomato soup?"

"I feel like it should be raining outside." She dropped her purse on the couch slid into a chair at the table. "This is my favorite blustery day meal."

James grabbed a couple of sodas from the refrigerator. "It was Mom's favorite, too. I think we had this just about every time it rained."

"Yup, total comfort food."

James sat down next to her. "Speaking of comfort . . ."

Missy winced. "It sounds like you're getting serious again."

"No, not really serious, but I do have a question. Things seem to be moving pretty fast between us, but for some reason I'm actually comfortable with it. I would have thought I'd be freaking out right now."

"Don't worry," she replied. "I'm freaking out enough for both of us."

"You?" James was truly surprised. "You strike me as someone who can handle just about anything. Even Will is afraid of you."

Missy swallowed the bite of sandwich in her mouth. "I'm not afraid of people like him. He's all bark. If you want to know the truth, I guess I'm a little afraid of *you*."

"You're afraid of me?" James almost dropped his spoon.

"Yeah, you." She turned in her chair to face him. "I can handle the physical stuff. I took my share of beatings when I was a kid, so that doesn't scare me. What scares me is the emotional crap. I've learned to just shut that stuff off, but then you came along and . . . well . . . for some reason I just can't. I actually cried last night."

"You cried?"

"Yeah, I cried. When that bastard called and said you'd been arrested, I cried . . . right after I threatened to kill him."

James took her hands in his. "Well, I'm glad you let him live until he had a chance to get me out."

Missy grinned. "If he hadn't got you out of there, we'd probably be sharing a cell right now."

James turned back to his lunch. "Remind me never to cross you."

Missy looked at her at phone and grimaced.

"Ah shit, I thought my calendar was clear today. I've got to get out of here. I have a client this afternoon and I need to get home and change. I can't waltz into the salon wearing the same clothes I had on yesterday."

"Don't they call that the walk of shame?" James joked.

"Who says I'm ashamed?" Missy gave him a kiss and headed for the door.

"Are you leaving now?" He asked, looking like a child who was about to have his favorite toy taken away. "You haven't finished your lunch."

Missy frowned. "Sorry, but I've got to run. I can't afford to be late. Where's the nearest bus stop?"

"I'll take you home," he volunteered as he jumped up and reached for his keys.

"No!" She fired back quickly. "You're supposed to lay low until you hear from that pig-headed jackass! The cops are probably out there looking for you right now."

James handed her his keys. "Then you take the car. I'm not going to need it anyway if I'm stuck here."

Missy pulled the big wooden door open and turned back to look James in the eye.

"I'll be back as soon as I can. I just need to grab some clothes and take care of this one client. I'll get the other girls to cover my appointments for a couple days, you know, just until this blows over."

"Do whatever you need to do," he said reaching down and kissing her softly. "I'm not going anywhere."

"Oh, you're going places," she responded. "Just not today."

James watched as she stepped off the porch and walked toward the car. Reluctantly, he closed the door and locked it after she drove away. He ran his hand over the large wooden door. Once again that door played a major role in his life. Again, it had become his protector. It kept the hounds at bay and locked out what might be a real threat this time, not just the imaginary ones his mother planted in his mind.

He also knew later that night, the door would open once more, allowing a special woman to re-enter his house.

His house!

For the first time James thought of it that way. This was his house now, and his life.

Chapter 19

Detective Carl Stiverson grabbed his chair and rolled it across the aisle. Letting out a grunt, the tall black man lowered himself onto the seat.

"You been here all night Doogie?"

"Pretty much," Will responded without looking away from his computer monitor. "I wanted to get our seller's prints in the system as fast I could. I need some charges that are going to stick on this bastard."

"What are you worried about?" Carl looked perplexed. "We got this guy dead to rights. He was holding the marked money. Hell, we even got the heroin. Ain't no way he's skating on this one."

Will turned his chair to face his partner.

"Come on Carl, it's a minor bust. As soon as the DA charges this asshole he's going to make bail and then disappear as fast he showed up here. I've got 48 hours to find out who this guy is before they bring the charges, and I'm going to use every minute if I have to."

"Well I hope you're having better luck than me," Carl said rolling back to his desk. "The buyer's in the wind. I heard he just walked outta here last night like he owned the place. I never had a suspect escape like that before."

"Did you actually arrest him and read him his rights?" Will asked.

"Just held him for questioning," he responded scratching the back of his head. "I didn't think I had enough on him for an arrest, seeing as how he wasn't holding the drugs when I nailed him. I was gonna see if he'd slip up, maybe give up his boss or something first."

"Then technically he didn't escape," Will said shaking his head. "He had the right to walk out and end the interview anytime he wanted."

"Hell of a way to end an interview." Carl sounded pissed. "Anyway, I've got the uniform that transported him on the way up. We're gonna sit down and see if we can build a face to go with the name."

Will straightened up in his chair, trying not to look too eager.

"I can help with that. I was in that alley too, remember?"

Carl looked at Will and nodded his head.

"Damn man, I almost forgot that was you. You don't look nuthin' like you did last night. Don't smell like it either."

"Yeah, I freshened up just for you, Honey", Will gave him a wink.

Turning toward his computer and logging in, Carl let out a sigh.

"Man, I hope you guys got a better look at this dude than me. It was pretty dark out there."

"I got a decent look in the light when he opened the door," Will replied quickly. "But the next time I saw him, his face was in the ground."

"Dude was pretty smart when the uniform brought him in." Carl sounded frustrated. "Kept his head down the whole time. I went through every frame we got off the cameras. Not one damn shot of his face!"

"What about when he left?" Will inquired. "Anything usable there?"

"Where?" Carl scratched his head. "We couldn't even find him leaving the God damn building! Some rent-a-cop took him to the bathroom and he just up 'n disappeared."

Will breathed an internal sigh of relief but fought to stifle a laugh at the same time.

"Maybe he flushed himself down the toilet and escaped through the sewer."

Carl grabbed an empty paper coffee cup off the desk and threw it at Detective Dugan.

"Smartass."

Will caught the cup in mid flight and tossed it back. Stiverson batted it away and then reached down to retrieve it from the floor. He studied the cup for a few seconds, turning it in his fingers, and then looked straight at Will.

"That's another thing," he said with a curious look on his face. "The CSIs went through every piece a trash in that shop looking for a cup with the name Jimmy Ray on it so we could match up the prints with this guy. They got nuthin', Doogie. Not one scrap."

Will searched his brain to come up with a plausible explanation.

"We had guys inside. Marco had guys inside. Maybe this Jimmy Ray character had someone inside too. They could have picked it up and walked right out the door."

"Maybe," Carl replied nodding his head. "But that'd mean this guy ain't just another mule if he's thinking that far ahead. Looks like we might have ourselves another new player in town. Where'd your CI come up with this guy anyway? You need to corner that boy and squeeze some answers outta him."

"Come on Carl." Will shook his head. "You know he's never going to tell me that. Besides, if I shake him down, I might lose him. No, we need to be happy with the one we got. If this guy pops his head up again, we'll nail him just like we nailed Marco. We just have to be patient."

"We'll see how patient we gotta be," Carl replied looking over his shoulder. "Here comes our boy in blue. Let's see if we can't build us a buyer."

Carl put his hand on the mouse and clicked through a few menus. His computer chewed on the commands, eventually bringing the facial re-creation software to life on his monitor. Will rolled his chair across the aisle to get a better view as Carl greeted the approaching officer.

"Officer Marquez," Carl said extending a handshake. "Grab a seat and let's get this circus started. Between the three of us, we otta be able to put something together."

The officer rounded up a chair from one of the other desks and rolled it up next to Will. As he sat down, Carl made the introductions, pointing first at Will.

"Jesse, this is Detective Second Grade William Dugan." Carl continued as Will extended his hand. "Doogie, this is Officer Jesse Marquez. He just transferred up from South Mountain a couple weeks ago, but he's been with the force about two years. Worked gangs mostly."

Jesse looked closely at Will's face as the men shook hands.

"I don't remember seeing you there last night. Are you helping because you've run into this suspect before?"

"I was there all right," Will answered trying not to give his cover away. "I was just working things from a different angle. Like I was telling Carl, I got a quick look at the buyer in the light."

"I think I got a pretty good look in the rear-view mirror," Jesse said as he sat down. "But he had quite a bit of dirt on his face."

"Sorry," Carl said with a smile. "That was my bad."

Turning his attention back to the screen, Carl pointed the mouse at a menu and clicked one of the options.

"All right boys let's start with the shape of his face. Oval look right to you?"

Jesse nodded but Will spoke up.

"Nah, it looked more round in the light. His chin wasn't that pointy."

Carl selected a more rounded shape, but the officer protested.

"No, when I saw him in the mirror, his face looked longer than that. I saw cheek bones."

"Really?" Will thought fast. "What kind of expression did he have on his face?"

Jesse thought for a moment. "Well, when I first looked up, I think he was smiling."

"That explains it," Will replied mugging a huge grin and pointing at his face. "See how the muscles bunch up in the cheeks when you smile? Makes your cheekbones look more pronounced and thins out your chin. Don't worry, it's a common mistake. Did you good look when he *wasn't* smiling?"

Jesse shook his head. "No, he buried his face as soon I said something. He never looked up again."

"Round it is," Carl said moving on to the next menu. "I just saw the back of his head when his face was in the dirt, so I'm gonna have to trust you on that one. How about the ears?"

"I saw those silhouetted in the light," Will quickly responded. "They were pretty round and stuck out a little bit. Sat kind of low, too."

Carl pulled up the round ears. "Attached lobe or free?"

Will thought a moment.

"Free, but they were kind of thick. What do you think, Officer Marquez?"

Jesse's body language spoke volumes as he squirmed in the chair.

"You know I'm not sure. I'm starting to wonder if I really remember any details about this guy's face at all."

"Is this your first composite?" Will asked, feigning understanding.

The young officer nodded. "Yeah. I've always been pretty good at picking faces out of a line-up, but I've never had to build one from scratch before."

"Don't worry, Jesse" Carl reassured. "You'll get better at it."

"Tell you what," Will volunteered. "I'll teach you some memory tricks. We can pull those details out."

Carl grinned. "Listen to him, son. This guy is really good at pulling stuff outta his ass."

Will picked up a pen and flipped it at Carl.

"Just shut up and pull up the eyes, ok?"

Carl clicked through to the next screen. Will turned toward Officer Marquez.

"Ok Jesse . . . can I call you Jesse?"

"Sure."

"Ok Jesse, just close your eyes and relax."

Jesse closed his eyes and listened as Will spoke a little softer.

"All right, now I want you to go back to the car last night. You're sitting in the front seat and you look in the mirror. Now freeze on that image."

"Ok," he responded, his eyes still shut tight.

"Look at the eyes," Will instructed. "Tell me, are they dark or light?"

Jesse squeezed his face up as he concentrated hard. "They look kind of dark, I think. I don't know . . . yeah, dark."

"Are they brown?" Will asked, knowing full well James' eyes were deep blue. "Black maybe?"

"Um . . . not black," Jesse responded sounding a little unsure of himself. "Brown maybe . . . yeah I can see brown now."

Will gave him a little encouragement to help cement the image in his mind.

"You're doing great. We have brown eyes now. Close together or far apart?"

"Neither," he replied. "They were pretty proportional to the width of his face."

"Good." Will kept him going. "Did he have big, round eyes or narrow ones? Remember, he was smiling so that might have closed them up a little."

"Right . . . smiling," Jesse parroted back. "They must have been kind of round."

"Did you get all that Carl?" Will patted the officer on the leg. "You can open your eyes now. You did good. That's exactly what I remember. How about you, Stiverson?"

Carl responded as Jesse opened his eyes and rubbed them.

"Yup, you guys are doing great. Like I said, all I saw was my flashlight on the back of his head. I can tell you he had a clean haircut, but that's about it."

"Well if you got the hair, add it to the image," Will instructed as he turned to Jesse again. "I'll fill in the nose and mouth. I remember those pretty clearly."

Will grabbed the mouse out of Carl's hand and quickly picked out a broad, crooked nose. He followed up with a thin, almost lipless mouth before returning the mouse to the control of his partner.

"Do you remember any distinguishing marks on his face?" Will asked.

Jesse closed his eyes once more and screwed up his face. "It's hard to tell. His face was pretty dirty. There were a couple of lines under his left eye, but I think it was just mud."

"No, I think that was a scar." Will seized the opportunity to drive the picture further away from his new brother's face. "I'm sure there was something there before Carl sat on him . . . like a burn scar or a birthmark maybe."

"Yeah!" Jesse responded excitedly as he opened his eyes again. "Like a birthmark!"

Carl added the new detail and saved the image. Making a selection from another menu, he sent it to a printer at the end of the cubicle row. Office Marquez returned his chair to its rightful place and retrieved the picture, handing it to Detective Stiverson. Carl looked it over and handed it to Will before turning back to his keyboard.

"I'll get this out on the streets," he said

hitting a few keys. "We'll see if we can't flush this guy out."

"Gentlemen, we did some good police work here today," Will said with a smile. "I present to you the portrait of *Jimmy Ray!*"

With that declaration, he proudly held up a finished composite facial image. The picture bore absolutely no resemblance to James McCarthy.

Chapter 20

James sat at his desk staring at the monitor. To any observer, it would have been obvious his eyes were not on the ever-growing list of emails populating the screen. Instead he just stared off into space. His brain had disconnected from his optic nerve, and instead focused on the picture in his mind.

The image of Missy's wet body pressed against his as the warm water from the shower head cascaded over them was permanently etched into his memory. It played over and over again in his head like a video stuck in a loop. Had it not been for the familiar 'ping' of his phone receiving a text, James might never have returned to reality.

He shook himself back to the present and reached for the phone, hoping to see a message from Missy.

Maybe she's on her way home, he thought.

No such luck. He deflated a little when he saw the name Willy D on the screen.

"Oh, for the love of Jesus!" James spoke out loud even though no one else was there to hear. "What does he want from me now?"

Another pound of flesh, Josh answered. *He got you arrested, but you never actually made it into a cell, right?*

"Yeah, but he did help me escape," James replied. "I'm sure there have to be some strings attached. I'll bet he's going to use that to pull me into some other shit storm!"

Wow! Josh laughed. *Drinking, fooling around in the shower with women, and now you're even starting to talk like me. Somebody's growing up fast.*

"Oh, shut up!"

And with that, James consciously turned off the voice in his head and placed his focus back on the phone. He opened the message center and reluctantly started an exchange.

WILLY D: Took care of things. You should be in the clear now.

JAMES: So the police aren't looking for me anymore?

WILLY D: You - No. Jimmy Ray – Yes

JAMES: But I am Jimmy Ray. How am I in the clear?

WILLY D: Trust me. I took care of it.

JAMES: Why should I trust you? You're the reason I'm a wanted man!

WILLY D: I'll explain later. Lay low one more day just to be safe.

JAMES: Explain now!

WILLY D: Mom's tomorrow night, 8pm.

JAMES: Fine. One more day, but that's it.

James laid the phone back down by the keyboard and tried once more to focus on work. He sorted through the list of messages in his usual fashion, answering some and deleting others. Halfway through his communications from Simon, he stopped. There it was again. With all the excitement in his life, it had completely slipped his mind.

Dear Mr. McCarthy,

I still have not received your answer to my query concerning the March conference. I realize this may be an uncomfortable subject, but I do need to respond to the request for an audience with you. These are powerful people in our industry and cannot simply be ignored. I need your decision soon.

I would venture to say this decision will have an effect on both your brand and mine. Please take this into consideration when formulating your answer.

I await your decision.
Simon J. Walker

James sunk down in his chair and leaned his head back. He stared at the ceiling like he was looking for something. He knew the answer couldn't to be found in the ridges and valleys of the white stucco surface hanging over his head. He finally leaned forward, placed his fingers on the keyboard and started typing.

> *Dear Mr. Walker,*
> *I'm sorry I have not replied to this request, but I wanted to have an answer for you before responding. I regret to say at this time I still have not decided how to handle this situation. I realize something must be done, and I am currently weighing all options. I will make my best effort to have an answer to you by the beginning of next week.*
> *Thank you for your understanding,*
> *James McCarthy*

James felt a little bit better knowing the pressure was off for a few more days, but at the same time he now had a deadline. He knew he couldn't ignore it any longer. He realized either Josh McDaniel or James McCarthy had to show up to that meeting. The only question became which man would walk through the door.

Those bigwigs are paying to see me, Josh observed. *They don't even know you exist.*

"Maybe it's time they did."

Look kid, I'm glad you're finally growing a pair, but are you sure you want to take that chance? Josh sounded a little concerned. *We're talking about your livelihood here . . . and mine!*

"Maybe I don't need you anymore," James responded. "Maybe I'll start trying some things before I write about them and then sign my own name."

That's all fine and dandy, Josh replied. *But until you build a reputation, you still need me.*

As James tried to formulate a response to his inner self, the pinging sound from his phone broke his concentration.

"Really?" James sounded irritated as he grabbed the phone again. "What the hell does he want now?"

His expression softened when he saw the screen. It was Missy this time, not the infamous Willy D.

MISSY: Heading home. Be there in about 20 minutes.

JAMES: Ok. Heard from Will. One more night inside. I'll start dinner.

MISSY: Relax. Already got dinner covered.

The next twenty minutes felt like at least an hour as James tried to focus on his work. Spending days on end inside the little house used to be easy for him. Now that he had a taste of the outside world, the space within those walls felt tight, almost claustrophobic. He caught himself taking deep breaths in an effort to open up the room.

The thought of Missy returning, if even for

a few hours, somehow made his confinement more bearable. When she stepped through the doorway the previous day, he felt she brought something with her. Missy brought joy and laughter, something he imagined hadn't entered that house since the passing of his father.

Hearing the sound of the keys in the lock, James sprang to his feet like a loyal dog anticipating the return of its master. He made it to the big wooden door just as it swung open. Missy struggled to push it with her foot. She held a cardboard liquor box under one arm, and carried a large tote bag in the other.

"What the . . ." James grabbed the box just before it slipped out of her grip.

"Your mother, that's what." She pushed the door closed and dropped her bag on the couch. "She called me to make sure you were ok. When I told her Detective Dickhead had you stuck here for a couple days, she asked me to stop by the pub."

James set the box on the kitchen table. "Why didn't she just call me?"

"She said she didn't want to chance waking you up after the night you had," Missy replied, shedding her jacket. "Anyway, she was afraid you might not have enough food in the house, so she loaded me up."

"That was nice, but it really wasn't

necessary," he said as he opened the top of the box. "I'm used to cooking for two, so I have a whole freezer full of leftovers."

Missy smiled and helped him unpack the box.

"Well, now you have more. The two on top are already hot . . . corned beef and cabbage. We can have that for dinner. She wrote cooking instructions on the other stuff."

James shook his head as he surveyed the pile of containers. "Did she think I was going to be shut in here for a week?"

"She's a mother. Get used to it."

Missy packed the refrigerator as James retrieved dishes from the kitchen and set the table.

"Grab whatever you want to drink while you're in there," he called back over his shoulder. "I'd offer to open a bottle of wine, but I don't have any. I probably wouldn't know what goes with Irish food anyway."

"I thought you wrote about the wines of Sonoma?" She said walking into the living room and retrieving something from her tote bag. "You had me ready to buy a bus ticket and hit the road after I read that one. You listed all kinds of stuff that went with each wine."

James screwed up his face as he tried to recall the memory. "Yeah that was over three years and a few hundred articles ago. Anyway, I think the Irish are more about beer and whiskey if I remember right."

"Then it's a good thing she gave me this." Missy said producing a six-pack of Guinness from behind her back. "I think she's trying to get you drunk again."

"Or you are," he responded with a grin.

"Maybe . . ." She pulled her other hand around, revealing a box of condoms. "Dinner first, dessert later?"

James' eyes about popped out of his head.

"Well, ok then," he said taking a deep breath. "I guess we'd better eat fast."

James headed for the kitchen, returning with a couple of pint glasses.

"I think these are the right ones for beer. I'm pretty sure the strongest thing that's ever been in them is lemonade."

They both shared a chuckle and sat down at the table. Missy poured a glass of stout for each of them while James served the food. As they settled in facing each other, he picked up his glass and held it up, motioning for Missy to do the same. He thought for a moment and then gave a toast.

"Here's to not having to eat alone anymore."

And to dessert! Josh echoed in his head.

They both took a drink and the expression on James' face changed drastically.

"Wow, that's strong . . . and really smoky!"

"Maybe we should have started you out on a light beer," she joked. "Try a little of the corned beef first and then take a sip."

He followed her instructions and noted the difference.

"That changed everything. The flavors really complement each other."

"Yup." She handed him a piece of the dense, crusty bread Margie had also provided. "You can pair beers with food just like you do wine."

"I guess I never really thought about it that way." He held his glass up to the light and studied the dark brown liquid. "I need to hit the web and do some research."

Missy shook her head. "Haven't you learned anything? Forget the stupid computer. I know a great place out by the football stadium where they have over a hundred different beers and just about any kind of appetizer you can think of. That's where you need to do your research."

James nodded. "That's what Josh would do, right?"

"Screw what Josh would do," she replied. "I'm talking about what James should do. Try a bunch of different beers with a bunch of different foods and then tell people what *you* think.

"And that's another thing," she added taking sip from her glass. "I can't keep calling you James. It sounds too formal. Can we just stick with Jimmy?"

He smiled at her. "You can call me anything you want, just keep calling me."

"We really need to work on your pickup lines," she said grinning. "But that was a nice try."

The conversation continued as they finished eating. James recounted the escape for Missy, hands flying in the air as he spoke. She was just as animated as she told the tale of the haircut and her new alliance with Margie. They both laughed when she swiped her hand through the air, demonstrating the head slap received by the street hardened detective.

After finishing a second beer, James stood up and began clearing the dishes from the table. Missy followed right behind him, lending a hand.

"I'll wash, you dry," she said handing him a towel. "So Willy-boy is springing you tomorrow?"

"Yup. He said he took care of things."

Missy didn't look convinced. "Just made everything go away, huh? Did he give you any details?"

"I asked, but he wouldn't tell me anything," James responded as he worked. "He said to meet him at Dugan's tomorrow night at eight. He'd better have a good explanation. I don't want to be looking over my shoulder for the next ten years."

Missy handed him the last dish and drained the water from the sink.

"I guess there's nothing else we can do about it tonight. You know what that means."

"No." James put the dish in the cupboard and hung the towel up to dry. "What does that mean?"

Missy walked into the living room, picked up her bag and headed down the hall.

"It means it's time for dessert . . ."

Chapter 21

Detective Stiverson entered the squad room carrying a large paper sack. As he sat down in his cube, he set the grease-soaked bag on a pile of napkins and opened the top. Carl dug through the contents while he addressed the intense looking cop sitting across the aisle from him focusing on his computer.

"Ready to get your nose outta that thing and have a little lunch?" He asked pulling out a silver foil container and holding it out. "I swung by Rito's on my way back from the psych ward. Mixed green burrito, enchilada style with a side a rice . . . just like you like it."

Will spun his chair around, reaching out to receive the big man's offering.

"Have I ever told you how much I love you?"

Carl just glared at him. "Man, we really need to find you a woman . . . one that don't hit below the belt!"

"She was *never* my woman," Will protested. "Anyway, she's someone else's problem now."

"Did you warn him?" Carl laughed as he unwrapped a tamale.

"Nah, I think I'll let him find out on his

own."

The two men both chuckled as they dug into the food. Carl reached into the cooler under his desk and dug out a couple bottles of Gatorade. He tossed one to Will before cracking the other open and taking a swig.

"Come on man," Will complained looking at the bottle in his hand. "You know I hate the blue stuff."

"Well when you start paying, you can choose the color." Carl swallowed another mouthful before speaking again. "Anything new?"

Will straightened up, made some muffled noises and started pointing excitedly at the mess covering his desk. He tried to swallow the huge mouthful of food filling his cheeks. Carl gave him a disgusted look.

"Jesus Doogie, you're spraying food all the way over here! Didn't your mama ever teach you not to talk with your mouth full?" Carl grinned. "Wait, I know your mama. If she saw you do that, she would'a head-slapped you into the middle a next week."

Will finally got his mouth clear.

"Dude, I got a hit on Marco!"

The overly exuberant detective started digging through the mass of paperwork cluttering his desk. When he finally emerged, he held several crumpled pages in his hand.

"You're not going to believe this shit." He handed the papers across the aisle. "I got several hits on the AFIS database. I *told* you this bastard had to have a past. He's got outstanding warrants in Seattle under the name Michael Corelli and San Diego has him listed as Miguel Montoya. You want to hear the best part?"

Carl held up the papers.

"I can read you know."

Will snatched the pages out of his hand.

"Here's the kicker . . . our big-time drug dealer? He's a forty-eight-year-old CPA from *Boise!*"

Carl grabbed the papers back. "You're fuckin' with me!"

"No, really." Will almost couldn't contain himself. "His real name is Albert Bernstein. This guy is a pencil pusher gone bad. He was under investigation for embezzling when he fell off the map. They caught him siphoning money out of some potato grower's co-op."

Carl let out a full-on belly laugh.

"You're tellin' me he split town before them potato farmers *fried* him?"

Will just shook his head. "There is nothing right about you, Carl. By the way, what the hell were you doing over at the funny farm?"

Carl turned his chair to face Will. "Your gonna *love* this one Doogie. I had to question some tweaker that was climbing the damn walls and trying to scratch his own eyes out. Said he was afraid somebody was after him. You wanna know who he was freaking on?"

"Let me guess," Will said with a confident smile. "Was it our middle-aged Jewish Idaho accountant?"

"Nope." Carl got a smug look on his face as he held up a familiar picture. "The infamous Jimmy Ray."

Will perked up like a dog who just heard the treat box open.

"Jimmy Ray? *Our* Jimmy Ray?"

"The one an' only!" Carl put the picture back down and continued. "Word seems to be getting around on the street that there's a new player in town—a player that brought the great Marco down and then pulled a Houdini and just vanished right out from under our noses. This dude was one of Marco's biggest clients, so he figured he might be next. Dumb ass tried to off himself by overdosing on his own product."

"You've got to be kidding me." Will scratched his head. "I mean, my CI just dug this guy up a couple days ago. No way the street buzz can be that high already."

"Believe it, Doogie." Carl looked at the picture on his desk again. "Story is those two gorillas our number cruncher had at the drop the other night are talking up a storm. After we cut them loose, they hit the street, jaws a flappin'. They were telling how this dude slipped out the back without leaving a trace of evidence, and then walked right through the walls of this very building like some kind a ghost. They're telling everybody this Jimmy Ray guy set their boss up."

"One bust and these two morons turn the guy into an urban legend?" Will tried to look concerned, but inside he was doing a happy dance. "I guess it's a good thing you guys didn't try to hold them when you picked up Marco. Maybe we can use that to our advantage someday."

"Yeah, well maybe Jimmy Ray is doing the same thing," Carl observed. "If he keeps feeding this fear, he really could take over the local trade. We already got one guy in the cage and another one in the loony bin. Could be a lot we haven't heard about, too. This boy's got some momentum already."

Carl picked up the picture one more time and studied it closely. He held it up to light and traced the outline of the face with his finger, then read the description across the bottom again. With a stern look on his face, he handed the picture to

Will.

"Are you sure this is the face you saw?" He asked. "Something just don't feel right. This picture looks Latino, but the name Jimmy Ray don't sound Latino."

Will made eye contact with the large black man sitting in front of him and leaned in closer.

"Well you don't look Swedish, Detective Stiverson."

Carl glared back intensely, trying to look as intimidating as possible. After a few seconds, the big man broke and rolled back in his chair laughing hysterically.

"Doogie, sometimes you kill me!" He said finally regaining his composure. "If anybody else said that to my face, I'd kick their lily-white ass."

Will grinned. "And just how do know what my ass looks like?"

Carl palmed his face and then rubbed his eyes. "Alright man let's get serious now. I'm telling you, something just don't feel right. We got us a picture of a short Mexican looking guy, while the street has him as a tall Caucasian dude. What video we did get looks like he's kind of average height . . . maybe five-eight, five-nine. Hard to tell. The dude was slumping his shoulders and hanging his head."

"Maybe the street's wrong." Will tried not

to look guilty as he built the lie. "Maybe we're talking about two different people. Who says the guy they're describing is the same guy we pinched? You said you thought he might have had someone inside, too. Maybe he smelled a setup and covered his bases. Could be the buyer *was* just a mule. The real buyer might have been the one that slipped out with the evidence you said was missing."

Carl didn't look convinced.

"Good story, but it don't explain how we lost the guy we had."

"Maybe he came back for his man." Will scrambled to salvage the situation. "You said the guy never opened his mouth, right? If you have someone that loyal, that willing to take the fall and not give you up, you don't leave him twisting in the wind."

"Maybe." Carl scratched his head. "Or maybe he decided to spring the dude before he broke."

"Yeah!" Will agreed almost a little too quickly. "Maybe he pulled the guy out so he could silence him. I'll bet his body's already rotting at the bottom of some old abandoned mineshaft up in the Bradshaws."

Carl just stared at him. "Really? Boy, I think you read too many crime novels."

"Come on Carl," Will joked. "You know I don't read."

"Unless you count comic books," Carl added.

"Listen, we can sit here and guess all we want but that doesn't change a damn thing." Will leaned back in his chair. "We deal in solid evidence and the only things we have going for us right now are this picture and Mister Albert Bernstein, CPA. Everything else is just conjecture. Our guys didn't see anyone else acting hinky in there except his muscle, and they didn't get a clear look at this Jimmy Ray guy either."

Carl gave a defeated sigh. "Did you get anything outta your CI?"

Will shook his head. "Not a damn thing. According to him, this guy was a friend of a friend kind of deal. You know how that shit goes. Nobody really asks questions in this business. The less you know, the less likely they are to find you floating in a canal with a bullet in your brain."

"So, you just handed off that wad of cash to your boy," Carl questioned. "And he handed it off to some guy he don't even know? I've never seen you do that before, Doog."

"I've never gone after somebody like this before," Will replied. "I wanted this guy bad. I figured I had no choice. At some point you have to take some chances if you want to get results."

"Yeah, but five grand is a hell of a chance."

"That's ok." Will smiled. "It wasn't coming out of *my* paycheck. I forged your signature on the paperwork."

"Asshole . . ." Carl turned back toward his computer. "So, what's our next play?"

"I don't know what you're planning, but I'm questioning a suspect," Will replied digging for papers again in his piles of clutter. "Me and Albert are about to have a serious conversation. After that, I'm going to give the DA everything he needs to send his ass down to Florence for a long time."

"Think he'll give up the buyer if we threaten to extradite him on the other warrants?" Carl looked hopeful.

"He's got nothing to give up," Will said as he stuffed a wad of papers into a file folder. "I set up the buy, remember? All this guy knew was some mule named Jimmy Ray was showing up. He didn't have a face to put to the name."

"He might have one now," Carl said pointing to the composite again. "He's the only one to look this dude straight in the face. I can throw together a photo lineup with some other drawings. Let's see if he picks our guy out."

"Fine," Will said dropping the folder back

on his desk. "But I doubt he's going to be any help. He didn't get this far by being a rat."

"Well, nobody connected the dots before either," Carl replied as he copied and pasted several faces into a new document. "He's got more on the line now. Maybe it's enough to get him to roll."

"We'll give it shot," Will conceded. "But I'm telling you now, there's no way I'm cutting this guy a deal. Would you trade a major player for somebody that might end up being nothing but a pawn?"

Carl scratched his chin. "Maybe we just drop a few hints. You know, dangle the carrot without making any real promises. Worst case he gets a deal here, but you still got three other jurisdictions waiting in line to get a piece of his ass. Bottom line Doogie . . . I want the buyer."

Will finally threw in the towel. He figured there was no way he was going to discourage his partner from chasing down every possible lead until he either found his prey or hit a brick wall. Maybe the photo lineup was the wall he needed. Will knew one thing for sure — none of the faces on that page belonged to James McCarthy. The only question was whether Mr. Bernstein would offer up a new face. It was a chance he had to take.

"Print it up, Carl." Will grabbed the folder

and stood up. "I'll run it up the flagpole and see if he salutes."

Carl clicked the mouse one more time and turned toward Will. "Already on its way."

Will headed down the aisle, stopping at the printer to retrieve the still warm page. He gave it quick look and then stuffed it in the folder with the rest of his documents. As he headed for the stairwell, he could hear Carl's booming voice.

"Break 'im down, Doogie! Break the man down!"

Chapter 22

Missy rolled over and reached across the bed, her hand landing on an unoccupied pillow. She groped around a little before opening her eyes. James was nowhere to be found. Instead of waking up to the new man in her life, she found only empty blankets. The heavenly smell of bacon wafted down the hall from the kitchen.

Sitting up on the edge of the bed, she did her best to bring her long, black locks under control by running her fingers through them repeatedly. Finally happy with the results, she stood up, let out a huge yawn, and pulled on her robe. Raising her arms in a long stretch, she yawned once more and ambled toward the kitchen.

She rounded the corner, happy to see the pajama clad, unshaven figure tending the stove. Missy walked up behind him and put her arms around his middle, squeezing hard.

"Good morning Sunshine." James sang out in a happy tone. "How do you like your eggs?"

"Scrambled," she said in a sleepy voice, still clinging to his torso.

James looked over his shoulder and smiled.

"Good, because I already broke the yokes. I

never did learn how to make over easy eggs."

"Coffee," Missy grunted as she finally released her grip.

"Already on the table. It's in the insulated carafe, next to the cream and sugar."

She pulled out a chair and plopped down. After dumping four heaping spoonfuls of sugar in a mug, she added the steaming black liquid and stirred until everything dissolved.

"Not really a morning person?"

He smiled from ear to ear as he delivered breakfast to the table. Missy yawned again and looked down at the plate in front of her.

"More of a night owl, but I could get used to this."

James sat down and poured himself a glass of orange juice.

"I hope the hash browns are ok. I've never made them before. My mother always wanted exactly the same thing every morning: two pieces of wheat toast, one scrambled egg, and one piece of bacon."

Missy looked down at the plate in front of her. The spread included two scrambled eggs, three strips of bacon, a nice golden pile of hash brown potatoes and a lightly toasted English muffin.

"I'm usually lucky to get a cup of coffee and

a Pop-Tart," she said as she poked at the food with her fork. "If I even get invited to stick around for breakfast."

James shrugged his shoulders. "I don't really know what proper morning after protocol is, so I'm just winging it here. Am I doing ok?"

"Um, I'd say you're doing a little better than ok," she replied as she took a bite. "You're treating me like I cured cancer or something."

"It was my first time you know." The smile finally faded a little from his face. "I just wanted you to know . . . well . . . I guess I don't know what to say. Thank you just doesn't seem to cover it. I know breakfast doesn't either, but . . ."

Missy set down her fork and took his hand. "Listen," she said softly. "You know I've done 'it' with more than a few guys, but there's a difference between having sex and making love. Last night was kind of a first for me too. Something was different, you know? I think it might have been my first time actually making love."

The smile returned to his face.

"Wow . . . I never thought in a million years I'd be somebody's first. Did I do ok?"

"Listen, mister OCD." She let go of his hand and gave it a playful slap. "You don't have to analyze everything and try to figure out how to make it better. We both experienced something new, and we both enjoyed it. Let's just leave it at that and let things happen however they're going to happen. Just roll with it ok?"

"You'd think after the last few days, I'd be better at just rolling with it," he observed. "Talk about things getting out of my control."

"You just need more practice letting go," she said, finishing up her coffee. "Have you got any plans today?"

"I'm just going to try to get some work done," he said looking over toward the den. "And I'm supposed to meet Will tonight at the pub."

Missy stood up and picked up their empty plates. "You really work for yourself, right? I mean, there's nothing that can't wait until tomorrow. I say we just get in the car and go somewhere—no planning, just head out of town for the day and see where we end up."

James nodded. "That sounds fun. I've never been outside of the Valley before. I'd pack up some food and drinks, but I don't even own a cooler. I never needed one before."

Missy walked up behind him and rubbed his shoulders.

"Oh, Jimmy. We have a *lot* of work to do with you. We can just get whatever we need, wherever we end up. That's the whole point here."

She gently kissed the top of his head and

turned toward the hallway.

"Now I'm going to go take a shower. If you plan on following me, you'd better get it in gear."

James jumped up from the table and eyed the dirty dishes in the sink. He looked back at Missy as she sauntered down the hall, hips swinging, and quickly fell in behind her.

"Dishes can wait!"

***

Missy stood by the car tapping her fingers on the roof impatiently. James finally emerged from the house carrying a canvas grocery bag in one hand and a rolled-up blanket in the other. He stuffed the blanket under his arm and fumbled with the keys. Finally managing to get the door locked, he turned and headed for the car.

She looked at him and shook her head.

"Really? You couldn't just leave empty handed, could you."

"Sorry, old habits die hard." He unlocked the car and tossed everything in the back seat. "It's just some bottled water, a little fruit and a blanket. You never know when the car might break down or something. We could get stuck somewhere for a while."

Missy got in and closed her door as James was buckling up.

"Some article you wrote about being

prepared?"

"Maybe . . . ok, yeah. I might have written one a while back," he admitted. "But I didn't pack everything on the list. Does that count?"

"It's a start." She clicked the seatbelt and looked out the window as he backed down the driveway. "So which way are we going?"

James stopped before the car reached the street.

"I have no idea," he said looking around. "I've never done this before, remember?"

Missy thought for a moment before raising her hand and pointed.

"Let's go north. I'm thinking lunch in Prescott."

"Really?" James looked worried. "There might be snow up there this time of year."

"Yes," she replied zipping up her jacket. "There *is* snow up there right now. If you've never left the Valley, I assume you've never seen snow, right?"

James shook his head.

"Only on TV."

Missy clapped her hands together like an excited child.

"Well then get ready for another first, because we're building a snowman."

"Great . . ." James sounded less thrilled than

his passenger as he guided the car through the city. "You'll have to give me directions once we get out of town. I've only been up I-17 as far as Carefree Highway."

"It's an easy drive." She squirmed excitedly in her seat. "You're going to *love* this! We can have lunch at the Hotel Saint Michael, and then do Whiskey Row . . ."

"*Oh God!*" James exclaimed. "*Please*, no more whiskey!"

Missy giggled at his reaction.

"Relax Jimmy. Whiskey Row is a place, not a drinking event . . . well, I guess it's an event for some people, but I think we'll just walk around today."

He breathed a sigh of relief.

"All I could picture was a bunch of shot glasses filled with different whiskeys lined up in a row. You had me a little scared for a minute."

"Whiskey Row is what they call Montezuma Street in front of Courthouse Square," she explained. "Story is there used to be about forty bars and saloons in that one block stretch. There's still a bunch around, but other stuff has moved in too — art galleries and little shops . . . you know, tourist crap. Sometimes the bikers get a little crazy up there on the weekends, but we should be fine. I mean, it's the middle of the day, in the middle of the week. Most of those guys are just weekend wannabes anyway. I'll bet they're all sitting in cubeville right now."

"Sorry, but when I heard whiskey I panicked." He shot her a sideways smile. "I guess my mom has me a little gun-shy."

"That's the first time I've heard you just call her your mom," Missy said with surprise. "You always call her your *new* mother or something like that."

James thought about his words, repeating them in his mind several times. He *did* call her his mom, no qualifiers this time, just his mom. The thought made him happy. He had a mother again. He looked over at Missy and spoke the words out loud this time.

"I have a mother again." He started to choke up. "I have a real mom . . . and a family. I mean, I've had a mom before, but I've never had a whole family."

Missy could see the emotion welling up in his eyes.

"You're just figuring that out? I know Mrs. Dugan isn't your biological mother, but I don't think that matters to her. You're as good as blood in her eyes. She was ready to do some damage to Will the other night when she found out what he had gotten you into."

"It isn't just her." James wiped his eyes. "It's all of you guys. Donny is like a big brother; at least I think he is. I've never had a big brother so I don't really know, but I'm pretty sure he's what one should be like. I'm not sure where Will fits in yet, but he took a big chance when he came back for me. He didn't just leave me there."

"Don't forget, he's the one who *put* you there," she reminded him. "He made the mess, and he needed to clean it up."

"I know that." James sniffed as he reached out and took her hand. "And then there's you. You've been really patient with me. I started out lying to you that night, but you haven't held that against me."

Missy dug through her purse for a tissue and handed it to him.

"Why would I hold that against you? Do you know how many guys have lied to me? All of them . . . *including* my own father. You came clean right away and you've been straight with me ever since. That's another first for me."

"We're just full of firsts." James wiped his eyes and blew his nose. "I guess I just feel a little guilty."

"Guilty?" Missy looked surprised. "What have you done to feel guilty about?"

"You know, my mother was my whole

world until a few months ago. When she passed, I thought my life was over, but look where I'm at now." He took a deep breath and looked out at the beautiful desert scene passing by. "I'm almost thirty-two years old and my life is really just starting. I feel guilty because for the first time I can remember, I'm happy. My mother's dead, I've replaced her, and I'm happy."

Missy looked on in silence for a moment, not sure what to say. Finally, she gathered her thoughts and spoke. Her tone was more serious than James had ever heard before.

"Look, I'm not very good with words like you are, so just be patient and listen. Life changes and we have to change with it. You haven't replaced your mother, and you never will. She is the one that made you who you are today, and I think she did a pretty good job. Sure she may have had her faults, but she taught you how to be a loving, caring person. Now it's Margie's turn."

She took his hand again.

"Think about it this way, did you have the same teacher every year in school?"

James silently shook his head.

"Well, it's kind of like that," she said stroking his hand gently. "It's time for you to move on to the next grade and she's your new teacher. She has something different to pass on to you. It doesn't mean your real mom is any less important, it's just time for some new lessons."

James squeezed her hand and smiled.

"That's pretty impressive for someone who's not good with words."

"Yeah." She choked up a little as she replied. "But I can't take all the credit. I have a new teacher, too."

Chapter 23

Shouts and laughter filled the air as Will Dugan walked through the door of the pub. The usual rowdies were gathered around the big TV, passing pitchers of beer around and yelling at the action on the screen. Lively music wafted overhead as people raised their voices, carrying on conversations over the din. A typical night at Dugan's Public House was in full swing.

The serious look on the detective's face was in sharp contrast to that of his older brother. Donny laughed, grinning from ear to ear as he served drinks and joked with the regular patrons lining the bar. The big man engaged with his happy audience, completely unaware of his sibling's approach.

Will walked up from behind and put a hand on his brother's shoulder.

"Have you seen McCarthy yet?"

"Jimmy? No, hasn't been here since . . . well, you know." Donny turned his head and pointed with his bearded jaw. "Mum's in the back, but I don't think she's gonna be too happy to see you."

"I guess I have to face her sometime." Will turned toward the kitchen door. "You might want to crank the music up. I have a feeling this is going to get a little loud."

Will walked through the swinging door and bypassed the kitchen, heading straight for the little office at the back of the storage area. He came around the corner and saw the small figure of his mother silhouetted by the bright white light of a desk lamp. Margie hunched over a pile of papers and receipts as she eyed each one carefully before making a manual entry in her ledger book. Will spoke as he walked up behind her.

"Aren't you ever going to get all this stuff on the computer?"

Margie turned and jumped out of her chair like she had just been hit by a bolt of lightning.

"*William Michael Dugan!* Are you *tryin'* to give your old mum a heart attack? You're gonna put me in my grave."

"Sorry." He took a step back like he wasn't sure if he should get too close. "It's not like I'm in any kind of a hurry to inherit half of this place."

Margie reached up and poked him in the chest with her stubby finger.

"You're gonna be lucky to get a bottle and two glasses right now. You dug yourself in deep this time, boy."

"Well, I managed to climb out and fill the hole. I'll get into all that later."

He reached down and hugged his mother.

The move was less about showing affection and more about immobilizing her arms before she could do him any damage. After releasing her, he turned his attention to the mass of papers covering the desk.

"I thought Donny was supposed to help you pull that stuff together and get it into this century."

She rolled her eyes as she sat back down.

"Your big brother's a fine barman, but he ain't got a head for computers. Running that credit card gadget is about the limit of his skills."

Will slid into the empty chair beside the desk.

"I really hate to suggest this, but have you talked to Jimmy about it? Sounds like it might right up his alley."

"That boy's got enough on his plate. Dealing with his poor mother's passing . . . and then there's that mess *you* got him all mixed up in." She looked disgusted. "Besides, I thought you had your knickers in a twist about him hanging around me and Donny."

"Yeah, well . . . I guess I might have been wrong about the guy." Will slumped back in the chair and crossed his arms. "I assume the worst about everybody until they prove me wrong, but that's what keeps me alive on street, Mom. It's what makes me good at my job."

"Well this ain't your job, it's your family." She gave him a stern look. "And Jimmy is family now, so you better get used to it. That goes for Melissa too, so long as she don't hurt him."

Will looked surprised.

"Now she's Melissa? And she hurt *me* — you're okay with that?"

"You deserved it, and you know it." His mother gave him a dirty look. "You came on to that girl like a dog in heat and when she shot you down, you landed her in a cell with a bunch a hookers for the night."

"*I* didn't arrest her," He protested. "She got caught up in a vice sweep. Wrong place, wrong time, that's all."

"Don't give me that malarkey!" Margie was heating up again. "You could of said something before they loaded her up in the wagon, and you know it. I bet she'd still be sittin' there if that nice Stiverson fella hadn't sprung her."

Will knew there was nothing he could say that wouldn't dig the hole deeper. Letting her cool off and changing the subject back to the bookwork seemed a better plan.

"Well, I just think Jimmy might be good with the computer stuff. We can run it by him when he gets here." Will looked at his watch. "I expected him to beat me here, but he hasn't shown up yet."

"He called a little bit ago." Margie smiled. "Jimmy and his lady are on their way. Traffic was a little rough getting back into town."

"Back *into* town?" Will didn't look very happy. "I thought I told him to lay low."

"Relax yourself." Margie waved him off. "They just went up the hill to Prescott for a little lunch. Jimmy got to see snow for the first time. The two of 'em even built a snowman on the courthouse lawn!"

Margie picked up her phone, swiped and poked at it, then handed it Will.

"They sent me a picture."

Will looked less than enthusiastic. "Great."

Margie snatched her phone back.

"Oh, grow up! You're just jealous 'cause she wouldn't give you the time of day. Both of them kids look happy. Have you ever seen that girl look like that before?"

"Never really paid much attention."

"That's a load a bull, and you know it." Margie didn't cut her youngest son any slack. "Anyway, I think they're good for each other."

Will stood up, shaking his head. "I'm going to go wait at the bar."

With that he retreated, leaving his mother

to continue wading through her paperwork. Will gave a quick wave to Miguel as he passed through the kitchen, and then headed straight for the only empty stool. Sitting down, he wadded up a napkin and threw it at the back of Donny's head to get his attention.

"I need a drink, Bro. Give me two fingers." He pointed at the lower cabinet behind the bar. "Make it the hard stuff out of Mom's stash."

"That bad, eh?" Donny retrieved a bottle from below the counter and slipped a glass in front of his brother. "I didn't even hear nothin' break."

Will lifted the glass and downed the golden liquid in one quick swallow. His face contorted as he slammed the glass back down on the bar and caught his breath. He could only manage to get one word out.

"Again."

Donny complied. "Greasing up your vocal cords, or just washing down the crow you had to eat?"

Will didn't bother to answer. He downed his second drink, making a face more grotesque than the first one.

"I hope that hits bottom quick." Donny pointed toward the entrance. "Looks like your pow-wow is about to start. The rest of the tribe just got here."

Spinning around on his stool, Will came face to face with Missy. James was right on her heels, shedding his leather jacket. Never one to be shy, Missy fired the first shot.

"Well if it isn't Detective Dumb-ass. Drunk yet?"

"I've got a good start," he responded sarcastically. "It should kick in pretty soon."

Donny reached across the bar and put a hand on his brother's shoulder.

"Keep it civil, Willy."

Will reached up and pushed the big, meaty hand off.

"I'm good Bro, but keep an eye on the little one. She has a tendency to get violent."

"What can I say," she snarked back. "You just bring out the best in me."

"Down, Girl." James stepped up and put is arm round her. He looked at Will. "Now that we're done with the pleasantries can we just get this over with?"

"Well, look who grew a spine." Will stood up and called back over his shoulder to Donny. "We're grabbing that table in the corner. Send over a pitcher of Smithwick's and a basket of chips."

Will led the way as they waded through the crowd. When they reached the table, he dropped into one of the chairs and propped his elbows on the table. James pulled Missy's chair out and took her jacket, placing it on the extra chair with his own before taking his seat.

"You're some kind of gentleman, too?" Will shook his head. "Are you trying to make all other guys in here look like a bunch of Neanderthals?"

"He doesn't have to try," Missy interjected. "Compared to him, the rest of you chuckleheads *are* a bunch of cavemen."

James held his hands up in the form of a 'T'.

"*Time out!*" He shouted.

Missy and Will both stared at him in stunned silence.

"You two need to grow up and stop taking shots at each other." James sounded almost parental. "Will, you might as well get used to seeing me around here because I'm not going away. I finally have some people in my life that care about me, and I care about them too. I'm not about to give that up."

Missy stuck her tongue out at Will from across the table.

"And you." James looked her straight in the face. "You need to stop stirring him up and calling him names. I know you guys have a history, but let it go already."

Her eyes widened as she straightened up a little in her chair. "Ok . . ."

James turned his attention back to Will.

"Now, why are we here? Why couldn't you just call me and tell me whatever you have to say over the phone?"

Donny walked up to the table with a pitcher of beer and a stack of pint glasses.

"So, did I miss anything?"

All three of them looked up at him from under furrowed brows.

"All right then." Donny smiled. "I'll just leave this here. Chips'll be out in a couple minutes. You want any vinegar or ketchup with 'em?"

They continued to stare at him without uttering a word.

"Tough crowd." Donny set the pitcher and glasses down. "Call me when the funeral's over."

Donny retreated back to the bar. Will filled the three glasses with beer and faced James. His serious look softened, as did his voice.

"I couldn't just call you. Some things require you to man-up and do it face to face." Will took a swallow from his pint and straightened his back. "I was wrong about you and I want to apologize. I shouldn't have showed up at your house and threatened you like I did, and I *really* shouldn't have pulled you into my mess the other night."

James looked down at the glass in front of

him, while Missy sat in stunned silence. His eyes slowly rose to meet those of the now contrite man sitting across the table.

"You know a month ago I wouldn't have been able to say this, but I think I understand why you did it." He looked over at the bar where Donny and Margie both stood by, trying to read the mood. "You do whatever you have to do to protect your family." He looked back at Will and smiled. "You don't have to apologize for that."

"Maybe not." Will finally dropped the serious look and worked up a grin. "But that business with the drug deal? I should have found another way to get it done, but I have to say, you handled yourself pretty good in there."

"Yeah, that's the other thing." Missy looked confused. "Why is it safe for him to be out in public now? Aren't the cops looking for him?"

Will started to laugh as he dug a folded-up piece of paper out of his back pocket.

"Oh, they're still looking for Jimmy Ray all right." He chuckled as he unfolded flyer. "But they don't know a damn thing about James McCarthy!"

He spread the page out on the table. Will laughed so hard he could barely speak.

"I kinda helped Carl and Jesse with their memories. Everybody's looking for a short Mexican with a birthmark under his left eye."

"What?" James grabbed the picture off the table and held it up. "Now I'm a short Mexican? How did you manage that?"

"It was all you, brother." Will recovered his composure. "You were slumped over and kept your head down the whole time. It also helped that it was dark, and you never opened your mouth either."

Missy grabbed the picture. "Where did the birthmark come from?"

"The big guy that caught me in the alley pushed my face into the mud," James recounted.

"You mean my partner, Carl? If you're lucky it was just mud."

Will started laughing uncontrollably. After a few seconds, Missy and James joined in.

"Seriously man," Will caught his breath. "You did one hell of job. I mean, I pretty much threw you in headfirst and you came up swimming like a pro."

"But what about that Marco guy?" James scratched his head and looked at the face again. "He looked right at me."

Will shook his head.

"He's not going to be any help, but I feel kind of bad for Carl. I had to bite my tongue when we showed the guy a picture line-up with this right smack in the middle. I got absolutely no reaction out of him. Carl figured he was just clamming up, you know, not being a snitch."

Missy felt the need to raise a point.

"What happens when this guy gets out of jail and sees Jimmy on the street?"

"Three other states want him when we're done." Will folded the paper up again and put it back in his pocket. "He won't be a problem."

"What about that scar you showed me?" James asked. "Are you going to be able to prosecute him for shooting you, too?"

"Oh, this?" Will pulled his collar to the side exposing the scar. "He didn't do this. Remember that fifteen-year-old kid I mentioned? This is where *he* shot me."

James scowled. "You told me Marco did that!"

"No, I said it was personal." Will straightened his shirt. "I never actually said *he* did this. I just figured you needed a little more motivation. You looked like you were starting to waver at that point."

Missy balled up her fist and punched Will in the shoulder.

"You're such a *shit!*"

James smiled. "You had me on the line and just needed to set the hook."

Will lit up. "You fish?"

"No." James shook his head "But I've written a few articles on it. So where do we go from here?"

"I say we go fishing," Will joked. "No, seriously, we had a shaky start here, but I think we might be able to make something out of it. You played that Jimmy Ray part pretty good—good enough to build a reputation on the street. I think we might be able to use that some time in the future . . . if you're game for it."

"It's tempting." James looked over at an obviously worried Missy. "To tell you the truth, once I got over the fear it *was* kind of a rush."

"One undercover sting and now you think you're James Bond?" Missy punched him too. "You don't know anything about life on the streets!"

"So, you can teach me," James responded rubbing his arm where she hit him.

A light came on in Will's head.

"You know, that's not a half bad idea. Hear me out on this one."

Missy and James both looked at him, and then each other. James picked up his beer and leaned back in the chair.

"What's not a half bad idea?"

"Well, you already have a reputation out there, but you don't have the experience." Will pointed at Missy. "She's got the experience, but she doesn't have your brain or your reputation. Put the two of your heads together, that's one hell of a resource."

"You mean work as a team?" James asked as he sipped his beer. "No throwing me into something unprepared?"

"Everything between us up front and out in the open," he responded. "But we'll still keep things on the down-low as far as the department goes. The less people who know the better."

James leaned over and whispered in Missy's ear. A huge grin came across her face as she nodded her head in agreement.

"Ok," James said smiling. "Under one condition."

"Name it."

"What kind of car do you drive?" He asked.

Will looked confused.

"I have a Jeep CJ-7. Why?"

James looked at Missy.

"It's not a right-hand drive Land Rover, but it should work."

"Works for me," she said with a giggle.

James set his beer down on the table, leaned in, and addressed the bewildered looking detective.

"I need to borrow your car…"

Chapter 24

James squirmed in the chair as Missy buzzed around him, scissors in one hand and a comb in the other.

"Will you please stop moving? You're going to end up with half an ear if you're not careful."

"This is a bad idea." James was visibly nervous. "I don't know what I was thinking."

She stood in front of him and put her hands on her hips.

"It's going to be fine. We've been over everything a million times. Just relax and have fun with it."

"I don't like this." He reached up and rubbed his stubbly chin. "My face itches."

Missy slapped his hand down.

"Stop playing with it. You'll end up with red blotches all over your face. It's just three day's growth. You can shave it tomorrow when this is all over."

After brushing the last few hairs away with a towel, she removed the cape covering the top half of his body.

"Ok, stand up and let me look at you."

James stood up and did a slow pirouette in

front her.

"Nice!" She smacked him on the ass as he turned. "I'd hit it!"

James returned the favor, chasing her down and giving her a quick swat.

"I know it's pretty nice out there right now, but we're supposed to cool off this evening" He looked over at the coat hook by the front door. "Maybe I should wear the leather jacket."

"No!" She answered sharply as she swept a pile of hair into a dustpan. "Your 'woobie' is staying home tonight. We agreed you're wearing the brown Carhartt Mom bought you."

"Yeah, I know." James pulled the new coat down from its hook. "It fits the image I'm supposed to be projecting."

"Exactly." She looked at the clock on the kitchen wall. "Where is Detective Dumbass? He was supposed to be here ten minutes ago."

James gave her a disapproving look.

"You said you were going to stop calling him that."

Missy reached up and gave him a quick kiss.

"Change is hard, Jimmy."

As James was collecting up his phone and wallet, the sound of the bell echoed through the house. Missy opened the big wooden door and admonished Will as he stepped inside.

"Where the hell have you been? You're late."

"Sorry, the Jeep was too clean. I took it out and muddied it up. Gives it a little more character." He tossed his keys to James. "You sure you're going to be ok?"

"I'll be fine." He handed Will the keys to the Buick. "Try not to wreck my car."

"I could say the same thing," he replied with a grin. "You've only been driving stick for a couple weeks. Last time you guys brought it back, I could smell the clutch for two days."

"Relax, dumb . . ." Missy caught herself. "I mean, Will. He's not going to break your precious toy. Besides, I'll be with him."

Will rolled his eyes. "Yeah . . . that's comforting."

James just shook his head. "Can we go now?"

All three piled out of the house and headed for the cars. Missy and James climbed into the dirty red Jeep, while Will opened the door of the old white Buick.

"You need to dump this old lady car," he called out over his shoulder. "It's bad for your image."

James fired up the Jeep and pulled away,

jerking and grinding as he shifted gears. Looking over at his girlfriend he couldn't help but laugh.

"I really am going to owe him a clutch when this is over."

They both had a good chuckle every time James got caught at a stoplight. Each time he started the bucking Jeep moving again, Missy gripped the handle on the dash with one hand and waved the other in the air like a bull rider. This only lasted for half a dozen stops before James began to get the hang of things, but the laughter continued all the way to the northern edge of town.

When her bucking bronco game ended, Missy came up with a new form of entertainment. She pointed out people in other cars and prodded James into making up stories about them. The tales ranged from lost love and romance, to murder and intrigue.

"You should write this stuff down," she suggested. "You're pretty good at making up stuff. You could even write fiction."

"I don't know if people would buy novels by Josh McDaniel," James replied. "His reputation is in the non-fiction area."

She shrugged her shoulders. "So, do it under your own name."

He smiled. "You've got all the answers, don't you?"

James seemed to be smiling a lot lately. His heart grew full every time he looked over at the bubbly, dark haired woman smiling back at him. Happiness was truly a new experience for him. He took it as a sign he hadn't managed to burn through all of the good karma he'd banked in his youth.

"I can't believe we're doing this." He took her hand in his. "You know this is absolutely crazy, right?"

Missy laughed and waved both hands in the air.

"Crazy can be a lot of fun! Just lighten up and roll with it!"

James pulled his phone out and handed it to her.

"We're almost to the restaurant. I guess I'm not getting out of this, so you'd better text Simon and give him the two-minute warning."

"Let the games begin." She punched in the message and hit send. "This is going to be a blast!"

James turned off the street and headed for the Valet stand next to the oversized double entry doors of the swanky restaurant. He quickly spotted the short, round figure of Simon Walker tapping his foot nervously as he craned his head from side to side like a falcon scanning for prey. Three men and two women, all dressed in suits, flanked the balding little man.

The Jeep came to a smooth stop directly in front of the stodgy lineup. The Valet ran up to the passenger side as James slipped it out of gear and set the brake. He jumped out and walked around the front of the vehicle while the valet helped Missy from her seat.

James confidently walked up to the man and slipped him a rolled-up bill as he took the claim ticket.

"Here you go." James put a hand on the valet's shoulder and grinned as he pointed at the crusty looking Jeep. "Try not to scratch it."

Missy stepped back to watch the fun as James approached Simon. The little man shook as he spoke.

"These are the people I was telling you about."

"Awesome," James responded. "Let's get this party started."

Mr. Walker turned and addressed his entourage.

"Ladies and gentlemen, it is my honor and privilege to introduce you to . . ." Simon paused and took deep a breath. "Mister Josh McDaniel."

Thank you for reading Killing Karma. If you enjoyed it, please take a moment to leave a review where you purchased this novel and look for the James McCarthy adventuress Catching Karma, and Cold Karma.

About the Author

Eldred Bird is an Arizona based writer of contemporary fiction. Using the Phoenix metropolitan area as a home base, his stories reflect the broad diversity of scenery and humanity found within The Grand Canyon State.

For information on upcoming books and projects, follow him on the web at:
http://eldredbird.com.
Or
Facebook:
https://www.facebook.com/EldredBirdAuthor/
Twitter and Instagram:
@EldredBird

Acknowledgements

I would like to thank the following people, without whom this book could never have been completed.

Debi Bird – Chief Editor, Graphic Designer, and Understanding Wife

Ed & Joanne Robinson – Content and Line Editors

Martin Fischer – Proofreader

The West Valley Writer's Critique Group of Avondale, Arizona – A special group of writers who took the time listen to me read every chapter out loud, and then told me what I *needed* to hear, not what I *wanted* to hear.

9 781735 383521